Finding Buddha

Finding Buddha

A Novel

Inese,

Thank you so much for supporting
my dream of Finding Buddha.

Best,

Jay Chalnick
6/13/15

Jay Chalnick

Finding Buddha
Copyright © 2015 by Jay Chalnick
All rights reserved.

This book is a work of fiction. Names, characters, places and incidents either are products of the author's imagination or are used fictitiously. Any resemblance to actual events or locales or persons, living or dead, is entirely coincidental.

ISBN: 978-0-692-35837-5 (Paperback)
ISBN: 978-0-692-35838-2 (eBook)

Cover photo courtesy of Monarch Studio.
Cover design by Scribe Freelance.
Author photo courtesy of Mark DeChiazza.

"You can't stop the waves, but you can learn to surf."
—JON KABAT-ZINN

For ZOC.

Las Vegas, NV

HOOVER DAM, NV

○Grand Canyon, AZ

Oklahoma City, OK○

HOLLYWOOD

PIZZA Flagstaff, AZ

Albuquerque, NM

BRETT & JULIE'S HOUSE

Santa Monica, CA

San Diego, CA

○Piacho Peak, AZ

○ El Paso, TX

MEXICO ½ MILE

Tijuana, Mexico

Tucson, AZ

KEEP
AUSTIN
WEIRD

MOTEL

Punta Cabras,
B.C., Mexico

Austin, TX

UNCLE MICHAEL
& AUNT MARY'S HOUSE

Columbus, OH

Westport, CT

HOME

Meramec State Park, MO

Roanoke, VA

Chattanooga, TN

Slim Goodies
DINER

New Orleans, LA

one

THERE'S A SIXTY-MILE stretch on I-10 that runs along the Mexican border. If you time it just right, you can catch an endless sunset as you creep northwest toward El Paso in perpetual twilight. You have to drive fast, though, as if racing the sun itself, but the view is intoxicating and compels you to keep pressure on the accelerator.

I have a photograph of our "First Mexican Sunset," as Bode later dubbed it, snapped at eighty miles per hour out the driver's side window. With nothing but desert on either side of the highway, it was unlikely to capture anything but the yellow sun and the desert vista dressed in gold. As luck would have it, I caught a road sign—a speed limit sign—dead center in the viewfinder. With the brilliant sky, sprawling clouds, and distant mountain range all in perfect focus, the sign post bends, lurching forward toward one o'clock, unsure whether it's supposed to stand still, say its prayers, go to sleep *like a good sign,* or join Bode and me in our quest to postpone tomorrow. In its indecision, the sign partially obstructs the sun but fails to mar the photo. Instead, the sun's rays strike the sign with the force of planets colliding, setting off an explosion of a thousand shades of orange.

I passed the phone to Bode for him to check out the photo. "Nice one," he said, handing it back.

Thirty minutes passed before either of us spoke again.

"Where are we going to bury Sophie?" he asked.

I looked to the rearview and smiled. Such randomness.

"Her ashes, I mean, where are we going to scatter them *now*?" he asked in reference to our previous attempt to scatter our golden retriever's remains.

"I was thinking Mexico. At Jorge's, maybe?"

"Okay," is all he said and stared out the window, as I recalled the ceremony that never happened.

I put off the ceremony at sea for months, complaining that it was just too soon, when in reality it was my fear of open water that was debilitating. I concealed my apprehension from Bode because I didn't want him to develop a similar fear. With Eliza gone virtually his entire life, Bode had very few connections to his mother, and I was determined to instill in him her passion for sailing, no matter how terrifying for me.

As the one-year anniversary of Sophie's death came and went, I decided it was about time. In another week, we'd be off on our trip, and who knew if we'd find another good sailing day before the weather turned cold. We headed over the sailing club in Westport on a Saturday morning and rented a Hunter 140. I asked Preston, the preppy teenager working the dock, if there was any reason why I shouldn't bring my phone to take photos, not mentioning our dog's ashes tucked away in my backpack or my intent to capture a small memorial ceremony.

"Well, the wind is pretty aggressive today," Preston remarked. "Do you know what you're doing?"

"No, not really, but I'm sure we can figure it out," I said confidently.

"Uh-oh," Bode muttered, not as quietly as he had probably intended.

I placed a hand on his head and added, "I did some sailing back in summer camp, so we should be okay."

Bode's eyes widened as if thinking, *We? I'm five. Don't bring me into this.*

"Well," Preston continued, "if you think you know what you're doing, go for it, but I'd recommend leaving your phone and anything thing else important in your car. You might capsize once or twice."

Clearly, my parenting skills were not on display that morning as I tossed Sophie and my flip-flops into the boat without even questioning how one capsizes more than once, how one rights a boat on his own while his son treads water for his life. After giving a push and waving us off, I could have sworn I heard Preston say, "See you in a bit." Once I discovered how to dislodge the centerboard from the rocks below, the wind swept us into the Long Island Sound.

"Are you sure you know what you're doing?" Bode asked as we raced toward the Atlantic.

"Sure, buddy, we're good." I faked a smile.

"Are you supposed to put that thing back in?" he asked, referring to the centerboard.

"Nah, we should be okay."

Not a minute passed before I recognized my folly. If Eliza were with us, there would have been nothing to worry about. She had been an avid sailor and owned her own vessel, a 1983 J/22, which I had winterized and stored at the club a few years ago. Most girls I knew from childhood had played soccer, volleyball or field hockey. Perhaps they cheered. Not Eliza, she didn't cheer for anyone. Eliza grew up sailing the Massachusetts Bay, and if there was any truth to the story, she was actually conceived on the water. At sixteen, she—or rather, her boyfriend's father with her onboard—took second in the Biennial Marblehead-To-Halifax Ocean Race, Division II, Class B. The achievement was a defining moment in Eliza's sailing career and the impetus for her lifelong passion for racing. Sadly, her passion lasted just ten years before her death.

Instinctively, Bode tightened the straps on his life vest. I resolved to keep the smile on my face no matter how fast or out of control we sailed; so long as he believed I knew what I was doing, we'd be fine.

Not a hundred yards offshore, a gust of wind filled our sail causing us to heel to starboard. With the back of my head nearly touching the water, Bode was lifted heavenward and clung to his portside seat. His mouth, like Munch's *The Scream*, was a deep, gaping abyss. I maintained my faux grin and held my breath, not wanting to take on any more weight to my side of the boat. Fortunately, we righted ourselves and lived to sail another day.

"*Woo-hoo*! That was fun, huh, buddy?"

"We need Mom," he said.

It quickly became evident that we weren't going to hold a memorial service at sea that day, but it was not until the boom swung back and clocked me upside the head that I decided we had enough sailing altogether. I seized the tiller from Bode—clearly, he didn't have a clue how to use it—and gave it a yank to attempt a one-eighty. Another gust of wind pounded the sail with a thump and threw me head over heels into the water. Rising to the surface, I saw Bode hanging from the portside of the overturned boat, feet dangling beside my head.

"What are you doing, buddy?"

"What should I do?" he squealed like a kid hanging from

monkey bars too high from the ground.

"Just let go."

He released his grip and dropped into the water.

I grabbed him by the waist and kissed him on the forehead. "Let's not tell anyone about this, okay?" I said, hoping it wouldn't become the defining moment in his sailing career.

Remembering the phone, I mumbled a few obscenities and patted the pockets of my cargo shorts to take inventory. The phone was still there but likely was toast. I felt my keys as well but could not account for my wallet. Perhaps it was in the backpack.

"Sophie!" I shouted. I twisted around and saw my flip-flops floating about ten yards away. Just beyond floated the backpack containing our packed lunch, blanket, and of course, Sophie's remains.

I considered the appropriate course of action. Do I stay by the capsized boat with my five-year-old? Do I leave him with the boat and chase down our dead dog? Do I employ my lifeguarding skills (acquired the same summer as my sailing skills) and hightail it via sidestroke with Bode in tow to retrieve Sophie?

"C'mon, we need to get Sophie." I wrapped my arm around his chest and abandoned the boat. Evidently, we were swimming with a current because we made it to the backpack with relative ease, recovering my flip-flops along the way. Unfortunately, when we turned back to the boat, it also seemed to find a current because it was more than a hundred yards away. Not bothering to question how that could possibly happen, I turned my attention to the shore and casually waved to Preston for assistance.

Safely ashore, Bode and I headed inside the boathouse to pay for the boat rental. Fortunately, the girl at the cashier hadn't the heart to charge us, or perhaps didn't know how to ring up a fifteen-minute rental. Either way, it was appreciated as my wallet was not in the backpack but resting on the bottom of the Long Island Sound beside my dignity.

Bode and I slogged over to the parking lot. I flipped open the tailgate of the truck, set the backpack on it and took inventory: no wallet; no cash; dead phone; wet towel, blanket, and lunch bag; safe and sound dead dog, securely contained in a plastic bag inside a plastic container. I stripped off the drenched cargo shorts I wore over my bathing suit and tossed them into the truck. With the towel and beach blanket soaked, we did a little dance—a silly attempt to air-dry our bodies—before hopping in the truck and driving to the public beach.

After a quick ride to Compo Beach, on the sand we spread our wet blanket, which needed no additional weight on the corners to keep it from blowing in the "aggressive wind." I removed the towel from the backpack along with Bode's insulated lunch bag.

A woman sitting nearby smiled but noticed something was amiss. Her friendly smile morphed into a compassionate frown as she watched Bode pour no less than a quart of Sound water out of the lunch bag. Bode noticed her, too, and gave me a little nod. I shook my head and fought to hold back laughter—my little wingman—and snatched the lunch bag from him. I removed a foil-wrapped sandwich and tossed back the bag with the remaining sandwich. The bread was damp but I pretended it was no big deal—it was all part of the sailing experience—because I didn't know how long it would be until our next meal with no cash or debit card. We worked up an appetite on our abbreviated adventure and it was not until our third bite that we spit out our sandwiches and laughed.

"Now what?" I asked.

"I don't know."

"Wanna swim?"

"Are you being facetious?"

I smiled at the word I'd taught him a week earlier. "Fair enough."

Observing us and perhaps overhearing our dilemma, the woman asked us if there was anything she could do to help. When she spoke, the wind blew her long brown hair into her face. A few strands stuck to her lips, which she gracefully pushed aside with the back of a hand.

"Thank you, we're okay," I said.

"Dad."

"Bode."

"Do you need any money? Would twenty dollars help? You can mail it back to me." She was already reaching into her bag while looking at us over her sunglasses.

"That's very sweet of you," I said, "but we'll be fine." Turning to Bode, I asked, "You want to get out of here, big guy?"

"Not really," he said with a grin on his face.

"Hubert," I called him by his given name.

"Hey!"

"Come on, grab your stuff."

Bode sighed as I playfully yanked the wet blanket from beneath him. I thanked the woman again, placed a hand on Bode's shoulders and nudged him in the direction of the parking lot.

Cars began to surround us, and I figured we were approaching El Paso after a nine-hour stretch of Texas highway. The sun was still hovering above the horizon and the hood of the truck, normally white, was smothered in golden sunshine. I was startled by Bode's voice after miles of silence.

"Are you thinking about Sophie?" he asked.

"I was thinking about our little sailing trip," I said, disconcerted at the amount of time I was daydreaming behind the wheel.

"We needed Mom."

"We sure did. She was a fantastic sailor."

"I liked that lady, though."

"What lady, buddy?"

"The lady on the beach, the one who offered us twenty dollars. She was very kind."

"She was," I said and smiled at him in the rearview.

"And pretty."

"Easy," I said, catching his grin in the mirror. "Ready for some dinner?"

"Yep," he said, stretching his little body and arms overhead.

The sun began its final descent as we exited the highway into downtown El Paso. We parked the truck in an area that seemed to have a few restaurants and found a Mexican place that had more employees than patrons. We ordered the homemade guacamole, prepared tableside, and the biggest cheese quesadilla either of us had ever seen.

"That's a big *cheesadilla*," Bode remarked as the server placed it in the middle of the table.

The waitress smiled and said, "*Muy guapo.*"

I smiled back and served Bode a huge triangle of quesadilla. "So, what do you think? Crash here or try to make it to Tucson?"

"I'm okay. How long is it, three more hours?"

"Five."

"Yikes."

"I know. But if we make it tonight, we can hike that mountain I was telling you about tomorrow. It's less than an hour from Tucson."

He offered no response but attacked his food, famished after the long drive from Austin with only one rest stop for fuel and snacks. Minutes later, as if no time had passed, Bode asked whether his mom liked to hike as much as he did.

I smiled. "She did. You know, we lived in the city for a bunch of years before you were born, so there wasn't much hiking to do except when we went camping."

"Did Mom like to camp, too?"

"Are you kidding? She was an awesome camper, just like you. She loved s'mores, though." I shot him the *only-kid-in-the-world-to-not-like-s'mores* look. "We'd get out of the city some weekends in the spring and summer to go upstate. You know that campground where we saw the bear a couple months ago? Your mom and I went there a few times and hiked that same mountain. That was a long hike, huh?"

"It wasn't so bad," he said. "The part with the long grass was tough."

It's funny what kids remember. He didn't remember the other family with two kids that joined us on the hike. He didn't remember wiping out on the steep rocks on the way down. He didn't even remember the awesome Mexican feast we enjoyed in town afterward. All he remembered was the long grass, a mere hundred-yard level straightaway on an otherwise strenuous four-mile trail.

"Yes, that part was tricky for you. Especially because you chose to walk *through* the grass and not on the path."

"Do not go where the path may lead, go instead where there is no path and leave a trail."

"Yes, my little Emerson," I beamed. "Never stop blazing trails."

Every night before lights out, I would have Bode read the Ralph Waldo Emerson quote I had fixed above his headboard when he was three years old. I stuck it up before he could read, of course, but after just a few nights of pointing to the words and reading it together, he had it memorized and would recite the quote as I tucked him in.

Bode flashed me a smile with a string of melted cheese hanging down his chin, confident that he'd finally used the quote in context.

"You know, the last time your mom and I hiked that mountain she was seven months pregnant with you."

"I thought she was sick."

"She was, but she wouldn't let it stop her from living. She was incredible, your mom."

A gentle smile appeared on his face as his gaze fell to his empty plate. I couldn't tell if he missed her, wished he had known her, or what. He simply went quiet for a moment. Was it possible to miss someone you hadn't ever really known? My heart ached for him, as it had for years.

Then he asked, "How far from Tucson to Pinnacle Peak again?" He served himself another triangle of quesadilla.

"Have I been calling it Pinnacle Peak? That's in Scottsdale, another hour or so north. We're hiking Picacho Peak," I said. "It's a little less than an hour from Tucson."

Crickets. And then, "Why not Pinnacle Peak?"

"Why not Pinnacle Peak?" I repeated. "Why not Mt. Hood? I don't know, silly, because it's not on our way." I scratched my head and smiled, wondering what difference it made to a kid who had never even been to Arizona, let alone either of the mountains in question.

With the sun finally tucked beneath the horizon, the temperature seemed to drop a good ten degrees. Back in the truck, I gave Bode one last chance to change his mind about driving to Tucson and started the engine on his command.

We drove for several hours in silence. Occasionally, I would stretch my back and neck to check him out in the rearview. He was sound asleep and wore a gentle smile. I have a photo of him with that same smile, standing in some walker he had received as a birthday present when he turned one. It was a silly apparatus, that walker, with lots of bells and whistles intended to keep him occupied as he roamed the first floor of the house. I have always loved that photo because of his smile and the way his arms were stretched wide, as if he was learning to fly rather than walk. His lips are bright red and glossy. Moments earlier, he had his tongue out and to the side, just like his mother when she concentrated on her work. I found it fascinating to observe similarities like that between Bode and his mother with whom he shared just six days. In that photo, you could see his determination, Bode so focused on learning to walk rather than on the walker's ignition key that clicked or the mirror that spun or the steering wheel's horn that sounded more like a clown's horn rather than a honk. He was so happy, so engaged, with his arms outstretched and grinning—*Today will be the day I ditch this walker.*

Glancing up to the rearview to see that precious face again, I allowed the truck to drift onto the shoulder. The tires vibrated on the grooved cement and a deep sound reverberated through the truck.

"Where's Mt. Hood?" he mumbled.

"What, buddy?" I looked up to the rearview, but he was sound asleep.

two

THE BUDGET HOTEL INDUSTRY has made great strides in recent years. Just ten years ago, I remember staying at these same chains, one sketchier than the last. These days every Suite, Inn and Express is trying to outdo the other—sheets that don't make your skin break out in hives, towels replaced before they become as thin as the sheets, continental breakfasts offering more than overripe bananas and Rice Krispies. It was competition at its finest, and for $89 you couldn't go wrong. If you did, it probably wasn't worth complaining about.

We served ourselves some juice and coffee from the breakfast bar and sat around a glass table with our duffle on a spare chair. We were in no rush but we were itching for the first hike of our road trip. Our two attempts to hike the Appalachian Trail in Virginia and Tennessee had been foiled due to torrential rain. Even driving was a nightmare those days, and I could only imagine how miserable we would have been trudging along in the rain, fog, and mud. We lifted our spirits those nights by eating pizza in our hotel room and mapping out our drive west.

Bode ambled back over to the counter to investigate what exactly constitutes a continental breakfast. He held a piece of whole wheat over the toaster, and I got up to help. He also selected a vanilla yogurt from a large silver bowl of ice and had me bring it to the table while he waited for his toast. As I sat watching him, I wondered what he made of this place. He stood in the breakfast nook of a hotel in which he had spent the night but surely hadn't any recollection of checking in. In just a few days I had become adept at the check-in process with duffle bag in hand and sleeping boy over shoulder. I had also managed to avoid knocking his head against doorways, since New Orleans at least.

Before leaving the hotel, I refilled my coffee, and Bode grabbed us a couple bananas for the road while I stopped by the front desk to check out and get a receipt for my journal. Walking through the sliding glass doors, we were greeted by crisp desert morning air and the glaring signage of five other competing hotels within a one-block radius. And I'd been worried we wouldn't find a room at one in the morning. Standing outside, Bode pointed to the mountains on the horizon and asked if we were hiking those.

"No, I think those are the Santa Catalina Mountains," I said.

"How 'bout those?" he said, pointing in the opposite direction.

"Nope, the Tucson Mountains," I guessed, now confused whether I had the two ranges correct. "Picacho Peak is about forty-five miles north."

"How far away are those?" he asked.

"Not sure, probably ten or fifteen miles," unsure of which range he was referring to. "Shall we?"

We hopped in the truck and within a couple of minutes we were back on I-10. I glanced in the rearview, and sure enough Bode had begun his daily meditation. He sat cross-legged with his heels touching the bottom of his booster seat. His palms were up, and the tips of his index finger and thumb were touching. His eyes were closed, and his face completely relaxed. There was a bit of movement to his mouth, as he got comfortable, and his lips formed a gentle smile. His body swayed with the movement of the truck, but he was completely at peace.

I don't recall exactly when Bode started meditating, but it was after Naja came to live with us. Najaree Wattana was our au pair from Thailand who'd been twenty-two when she arrived, spoke four languages, and was quick to fall in love with Bode. Whether it was Bode's preschool teacher or Naja who initially taught him how to mediate, I'm not sure, but Naja encouraged it and made it part of his daily routine. On occasion, I would ask Bode what he thought about while meditating, and he'd say nothing. Literally, "Nothing." If I pressed him for an answer he would say, "If you're thinking, you're doing it wrong."

I was on the train by the time Bode woke up most mornings, so I typically didn't see him meditate except on the weekends when after breakfast he would disappear for twenty minutes or so. Some days he would meditate longer than others, and he found it easy to meditate anywhere—his bedroom, the living room, the couch, the floor. I always assumed people who meditated were strictly regimented in their practice, but Bode seemed relaxed and at ease wherever he was. I once checked in on him during bath time to see if he'd drowned, he was so quiet, but he was sitting up, cross-legged, and meditating in the lukewarm water, long after the last bubble burst.

Whenever friends of mine caught wind of Bode's meditation practice, they were astonished. *How do you get him to sit still? What does he think about? What does a five-year-old have to meditate about?* "He meditates about nothing," I once responded, but that only initiated a circular discussion. Although these questions came from some of my closest friends, I couldn't help but feel that if they needed to ask what someone meditated about, they could probably benefit from a meditation practice themselves.

I was a bit surprised at first, too, but back when Bode started meditating I figured it was simply something his preschool teacher had implemented to get the kids to sit still for a few minutes. It seemed sensible to me. While I don't recall giving much thought to whether other children were meditating in their own homes, I found no reason to inhibit Bode's practice. Occasionally, I would sit beside him and meditate myself, but it never stuck as part of my daily routine. On the rare occasion I attended a yoga class, I found the ten minutes during *savasana* sufficient to clear my head. Bode evidently got much more out of meditation than I ever did, and his practice had become as routine as brushing his teeth.

"Do you think Sophie incarnated yet?"

Startled, I looked up. "I thought you were meditating."

"Finished," he said, gazing out the window.

I smiled and flicked the blinker before passing an old Camry doing fifty in the left lane.

"So?"

"So what?" I asked.

"Do you think Sophie incarnated yet?"

"Do I think she has *reincarnated*? I don't know. I think her spirit is all around us."

"Like Mom's?"

"Exactly. I think her spirit's with us, but I'm not sure if she has reincarnated yet. I'll feel much better after we scatter her ashes, let her be free and all."

"Where is she?"

"Sophie? She's in the trunk," I said and then considered how absurd it sounded. "In the back, not the trunk." As if being packed away in the back of the truck along with our luggage and gear was any better.

"Are we going to get another dog?"

"I'd like to. But we'll have to see once I start my new job. We'll probably want to ask Naja what she thinks because we'll need her help, no?"

"Yeah, probably," he agreed.

I looked at him in the mirror and flashed a smile. Bode and I had established our own language over the years with various sounds, expressions and smiles. He knew exactly what my smile meant and grinned in return.

We arrived at Picacho Peak State Park just before nine. It was still early, but the sun was out in full force and the dashboard thermometer read 82 degrees.

"What do you say?"

Bode unbuckled his belt and flipped around to search the back for our water packs. He stretched over the back seat and with his rear end nearly touching the roof he reached for the packs. By the time he got hold of one that was squeezed between our tent and the window, I had the tailgate open and found the other.

"You ready, handsome?" I said.

"Ready, Matthew!"

"It's Dad to you, Hubert," I said, knowing how much he loved his given name, and ran my hand through his mop of hair.

After putting Bode to bed the previous night, I had surfed the web to read up on Picacho Peak. It had been quite some time since I climbed it with my fraternity brothers, and I wanted to get reacquainted. One site described the 3,374-foot mountain as "an iconic looking rock formation" just off I-10 between Tucson and Phoenix, which is certainly true. It's hard to ignore the uniquely shaped 1,500-foot peak that had been used as a natural navigation beacon for Native Americans for centuries.

I remembered the Hunter Trail as being relatively challenging back in college when I was a confident and cocky nineteen-year-old. I have a picture of me standing proud at the summit, arm and arm with Brett, my fraternity brother and, later, best man. We both had our opposite arms extended in the air, giving the camera a hang loose sign. Incredibly, I wore a pair of worn-out Timberlands with no socks, and there was just a small bottle of water sticking out of the pocket of my cargo shorts. Although Bode had hiked a number of mountains back home, this was no doubt going to be the most challenging for him. After reading up on the hike the night before, I didn't need the trailhead sign to remind me of the dangers: *Not recommended for children under 10.*

"You sure you're ready for this?" I asked, knowing very well what his response would be.

"Yeah, why?"

"Because the sign says this trail is not recommended for kids under ten. There are other trails we could take."

As always, I downplayed the challenges associated with our excursions. As a firm believer that fear hinders performance, in every aspect of life, the less Bode feared, the more he would try, and the more he would accomplish as a result. I figured I could (and always did) tell him how crazy our last hike or rock climb or canoe trip had been after the fact. Perhaps that makes me a bit sadistic (Is there a spectrum for sadistic behavior?), but my intentions were always wholesome.

"No way, I want this one," he said.

The trail was just over two miles to the summit but had plenty of scrambling and hand-over-hand climbing. At just under four feet tall, Bode was small but as most climbers know, tall isn't necessarily a good thing. Strength and balance on the other hand is, and pound for pound Bode was probably stronger than me. While I silently watched his footing, I doubted the vertical climbs would give him much trouble.

At half past nine, amidst a few looks of disbelief from other hikers, we set out from Barrett Loop on the north side of the mountain. As various websites warned, the beginning of the trail was a steep and twisting climb up the rocky *bajada* that flanked the mountain. It was a welcoming shock to our systems and got our hearts beating for the first time after nearly a week of driving. Out of breath, we took a water break among more funny looks from two couples doubled-over beside a bench.

We caught our breath and after posing for a photo, continued the trek. The view was already spectacular, but we hurried on, excited to reach the summit. We approached a very steep downward sloping section on the backside of the mountain. The steel posts and cables created handrails, but they didn't remove the element of danger or exposure to the cliff. At this point, I had Bode follow me, thinking it would be better for me to be downhill from him in the event one of us slipped. Of course, if either of us slipped *sideways*, there was nothing preventing us from falling off the mountain. Several of the steel posts wiggled as we clung to the cable, and my knees quivered. After several minutes of precarious footing and adrenaline-pumping tension, the trail finally bottomed-out and we made it to where the longer, but less aggressive Sunset Vista Trail joined the Hunter Trail.

"You okay?" I asked with the same calm in my voice as on the day of our botched sailing adventure.

"Uh-huh," gasped Bode, out of breath but standing upright.

"Drink some water. We're actually not far from the summit, but it's going to get a bit hairy."

We began our final push to the top. There was one more precarious section with the rock wall on our right and full exposure to the left. The trail narrowed, and the only way forward was over a fifteen-foot long wooden plank, just eighteen inches wide. I had Bode go first and followed in step. We walked slowly and deliberately, dragging our fingers on the cliff to the right, and safely reached the other side. Another hundred meters or so of gentle switchbacks, and we arrived at the summit.

The view was breathtaking. Though I had been there before, I did not recall appreciating the landscape nearly as much as I did this time around. The sky was clear and we could see for miles in each direction. We stood high above the desert floor, two emperors presiding over an army of saluting saguaro cacti.

Back at the trailhead after our descent, I snapped a photo of a beaming Bode pointing to the sign—*Not recommended for children under 10*. Sweat matted his hair to his forehead, and I caught a rare glimpse of his eyes as they sparkled like gems in the sunlight. Back at the truck, we sat on the tailgate and kicked off our shoes. Bode reached over the back seat to grab the two bananas from breakfast and tossed me one. We ate warm bananas and almonds and discussed our plan. It was just after one, and I saw no reason why we couldn't make it to San Diego by evening.

three

WE DROVE ABOUT FOUR HOURS before stopping at In-N-Out Burger in El Centro, California. I had been looking forward to paying a visit to the burger joint since we first planned to drive cross-country. That might sound crazy—putting a fast-food restaurant on your list of things to do—unless, of course, you have ever been to an In-N-Out Burger. Despite my best effort to entice him to try one of their burgers, Bode passed. Perhaps I spilled the beans about the secret menu too soon, but I didn't have the heart to withhold such prized information.

"Just be sure to whisper your order," I said.

The server gave Bode a wink after he ordered his grilled cheese and looked to me for the rest of the order. I ordered a Double-Double "animal style" and both our fries "well done," two more not-so-secret secret menu items. Curiously, I got a wink, too.

"How far to San Diego?" Bode asked, taking a seat at the only empty table.

"Just two hours. Are you excited?"

"Yep. Where are we staying tonight?" he asked, just as our number was called.

"That was quick," I said and stood up to retrieve our order. "I was thinking we should stay some place decent since we'll be camping for the next few days," I said when I returned.

"Okay."

"You're very easy to please, mister." I took out the phone and Googled *Marriott Coronado, CA* while picking at some fries and tapped on the Coronado Island Marriott Resort & Spa. I would have rather stayed up in North County, but Coronado was less of a detour on the way to Baja. I called the hotel's main switchboard and booked a room using rewards points.

"We're all set, buddy. Are you thinking what I'm thinking?"

"Pizza in bed and night swimming?"

I smiled and dug into my burger.

When we stood to leave, our legs ached, and we exaggerated our moans as we hobbled to the truck. We still had a few hours to Punta Cabras the next day, but San Diego felt like a huge milestone in our journey. Three thousand miles is a long way, especially when your copilot is more than a decade away from sharing the driving duties. I was looking forward to a few days rest on the beach.

As I started the truck, I looked at Bode in the rearview and asked if he was sure he didn't want to drive this leg.

"Facetious."

I laughed, put the truck in reverse, and Bode asked for the phone. We kept a bunch of games and movies on it like *E.T.* and *The SpongeBob SquarePants Movie*. Bode absolutely refused to use the ear buds, so I taught him how to turn the volume down after opening the various apps. He made a habit of telling me that he's on the case each time he opened a new app that wouldn't let him lower the volume until the title screen vanished.

"I got it, I got it," he said after opening some motocross racing game with an obnoxious electric guitar intro.

I smiled in the mirror and got ready for my game: guessing which app he'd opened. He played a few games with nearly indistinguishable music before firing up *E.T.*, a film I must have seen a thousand times.

By the time Elliott discovered E.T. inside the shed, we were passing through El Cajon, just twenty minutes outside San Diego. I was anticipating the dialogue in the movie when Bode asked, "Dad, how do you know Jorge again?"

"Jorge!" I loved saying the name. It reminded me of Baja and always made me smile. "Jorge is an old friend. I met him in college when Uncle Brett and I went down to Punta Cabras for the first time."

"Where is it?"

"Punta Cabras? A few hours south of San Diego in Baja California."

"I thought you said Baja was in Mexico."

"You're very smart, buddy. Yes, Baja is in Mexico. Baja California is the name of the state, like Connecticut in the U.S. People usually just call it Baja.

"The first time we went, Brett and I got a little lost because it was dark by the time we arrived. We knew Punta Cabras was a few miles north of a town called Eréndira but we couldn't find it in the dark. We drove around for a while but finally gave up and spent the night in Eréndira at a hostel called Coyote Cal's. It's still there and I'm friendly with the owner. You'll meet him."

"Jorge?"

"No. Rick."

"Oh. Hey Dad?"

"Yeah, buddy?"

"What's a hostel?"

"A hostel is like a cheap hotel for travelers. It's got the bare bones, a small bed, and a community bathroom. It wasn't much, but it was all we needed. Rick, who runs the place, pointed us to Punta Cabras the next morning. It was only a few miles up the coast but would have been impossible for us to find at night. You have to drive on a dirt road that turns into sand dunes. There was just one tent set up, but it was enough to give us an idea of where we could camp. We parked the car and hit some epic waves before setting up the tent. It was incredible, the best session either of us had ever had. And the best part was we had the entire ocean to ourselves."

"What about Jorge?"

"When we finished surfing, we climbed the bluff and found this old man leaning against the front of the car with a great big, toothless smile on his face, looking as if he had just witnessed the best surf session *he'd* ever seen."

"Jorge."

"Exactly. He had the tannest skin and his face had more wrinkles than a Shar Pei."

"Shar Pei?"

"Mr. Wrinkles," I said, referring to our neighbor's dog back home. "So, Jorge introduced himself. He's not actually missing all his teeth, just the middle ones on top. He said he lived just a few hundred meters away with his wife and son, and he wanted to welcome us. He hung out while we set up our tent and said if there was anything we needed—firewood, beer, anything—he'd be happy to help. We asked how would we find him, and he said he'd be around. And he was. Anytime we needed him, he appeared."

"He has a son?" Bode asked, perhaps hoping for a companion.

"Yeah, but he doesn't live there anymore. I drove him and his mom to Los Angeles the next year. It's a long story, but he and his mom live in L.A. now."

"Not with Jorge?" he asked, confused.

"Like I said, it's a long story. But you know the iPad we bought for him? It's going to help him see them all the time now."

"Facetime?"

"Yep. He will be able to go to Coyote Cal's to call his family now. And us."

"That's nice." A moment later he said, "But I don't understand why his wife and son left him."

"I know, buddy. I'll explain it to you later. Just know that they are happy and doing well."

"Even Jorge?"

"Yes, even Jorge," I said, not entirely certain. "He has a dog, you know."

Bode perked up a bit.

"She's pretty old now, but she's beautiful."

"What kind?"

"A black Lab. Her name's Bella. I adopted her for Jorge before one of my visits senior year. The previous time I saw Jorge, I could tell he missed his last dog. I felt bad because you could tell how much he'd loved that animal. So, a couple days before my next visit, I went to a local shelter and found Bella. She was only three or four months old, such a cute pup. I signed some papers, paid for her last round of shots, and bought a ton of food and treats for her. A couple days later, I brought her to Baja. If you could've only seen Jorge's face—you could have kicked a field goal through those teeth. Anyway, you'll meet Bella tomorrow. She must be twelve or thirteen by now."

"How often did you visit Jorge?"

"A bunch of times. Maybe ten? A lot of my friends would go away or visit their families over spring break or Thanksgiving. After Grandma and Grandpa died, I didn't have much reason to go home, so I would head down to Baja. It was a lot of driving for a normal weekend, but I'd go down most three- and four-day weekends. Each time, I'd try to bring him a little present—some clothing or scotch or something."

"Yuck."

"This one time I brought him a bunch of wood and nails. His mattress was on the floor, so I helped him build a platform so he didn't have to sleep on the ground."

"That was nice."

"You haven't seen the platform," I laughed. "Hey, buddy, see those buildings? That's downtown San Diego. We're going to drive right through it and over a bridge to Coronado. Let's charge the phone for a bit. And remind me tomorrow to charge the iPad for Jorge."

The hotel was easy to find—you could actually see it off to the right while crossing the Coronado Bridge. We didn't get a view of the San Diego Bay, but as luck would have it our room faced west, and we caught the tail end of a fantastic sunset. While Bode was in the shower, I ordered room service and sat on the balcony with my journal. The sliding glass door opened, and the little man walked out.

"What are you doing, naked boy? Get dressed."

"What should I wear?"

"Put on your swimsuit. We're hot tubbing after dinner, aren't we?"

As Bode walked back into the room, there was a knock at the door.

"Food's here, buddy, better hurry."

He started tossing articles of clothing from our duffle in an attempt to find his bathing suit. I goosed him as I walked to the door.

"Hey!"

I opened the door, and the room service waitress stood outside with a cart on wheels. I suppressed a laugh and stepped aside.

"Hey!" shouted Bode, still naked. "Dad!" He covered himself with his bathing suit that he found in the nick of time.

"Oh my goodness, I'm so sorry," cried the waitress, blushing.

"Don't worry about it," I laughed. I took the billfold from her, signed the tab, and handed it back.

"Thank you," she said. "I'm so sorry."

I smiled and closed the door behind her, turning just in time to thwart Bode's attack. I picked him up and tossed him on the bed and tickled him until he cried uncle.

"You got a salad?" Bode asked when we sat down to dinner and uncovered the platters.

"Yeah, we haven't been eating too healthy, so I figured we'd have a salad with the pizza. I ordered extra mushrooms. You can put some on your pizza, too."

We broke tradition on account of the sunset and ate on the balcony. They didn't put the mushrooms on the side as I had hoped so Bode picked away at them.

"You know, Dad, if you try them seven times, you're gonna like 'em," he said, stuffing his face with a few.

"Very funny, buddy." He was trying to use my own trick against me. When he was younger and would cringe at the taste of something on his plate, I would play it cool by telling him not to worry, he'll like it by the seventh try. It was my scheme to make him eat his vegetables while planting the seed, if you will, that one day he would actually like them. Truth be told, my little trick exceeded my wildest expectations. "I've tried mushrooms more than seven times, buddy, and I still can't stomach them."

As we ate, the sky changed from blue and orange to yellow and red before turning dark. Something about the way Bode picked the mushrooms from the salad between us reminded me of Eliza on our honeymoon. Although he couldn't see it, he was just like his mother in so many ways. People who didn't know Eliza had told me that he looked and acted exactly like me but I knew better; he was all Eliza.

"Are you thinking about Mom?" he asked, placing mushrooms onto his pizza.

"How do you do that?" I asked.

"You were twirling your ring again."

I smiled and slowly nodded my head.

"Why do you still wear it?" he asked, biting into his pizza.

"My ring? I don't know. Because I feel like I'm still married. I feel like—"

"It's okay for you to, you know . . ." his voice trailed off.

I wasn't sure I knew what he was saying. If it were coming from a friend, sure, it would make sense. But he wasn't even six years old. How could he possibly know that it was time for me to move on?

"I don't want to talk about this right now, okay, buddy?"

"But, Dad—"

"Bode, please. Let's finish up so we can hit the jacuzzi, okay?"

We finished the meal under the yellow glow of our balcony light. I wouldn't admit it to him until much later, but I considered what he was trying to say for the rest of dinner and well into the night.

four

IT WAS NEARLY ELEVEN when we finished swimming. The pool was heated—not that it needed to be—but we were grateful because it felt cold each time we hopped into it from the jacuzzi. We weren't the only people at the pool that night, but we were the last to leave. Foreheads touching in the pool, we whispered our plan to hold another cannonball competition when everyone left.

"When is everyone going to leave?" I whispered, feigning urgency.

"I don't know," he replied, *sotto voce* as well.

"Tell them to leave."

"I can't."

"But the diving board is calling for us."

"I know."

"Tell them to go."

"Daddy, you're being silly."

"I can't wait any longer! I'm gonna jump."

"Daddy, no!"

Instead, I grabbed him and tossed him high into the air, catching him just as he hit the water. He squealed with delight and asked me to do it again and again. We passed the time alternating between pool and jacuzzi until everyone else had gone and we had the pool—and diving board—to ourselves.

Our tradition of night swimming began the previous Christmas Eve when I booked a room at the local Marriott. With no family nearby, I figured we'd grab dinner at the hotel restaurant and take advantage of the indoor pool. We ended up ordering room service and eating dinner in bed before sneaking to the pool after hours. After racing back and forth between pool and jacuzzi and performing one too many cannonballs, the night manager, who was clearly unhappy about working Christmas Eve, politely asked us to go back to our room. Sent to bed before we were ready, Bode whipped out one of the wrapped presents I had packed away in our bag. Knowing what it was—a new chess set—I allowed him open it early, and we played until well after midnight.

Bode was just a beginner, but he understood the movement of all the pieces, as well as the value of each. Since he was just learning strategy, I had my way with him and fooled him with simple traps to capture his queen or rook. He was quick to catch on, however, and learned to keep his finger on top of pieces longer, double and triple checking to see whether he was exposed. The only chess we had with us on our trip was on the phone, but neither of us enjoyed playing on the small screen.

The jacuzzi at the Coronado Island Marriott was exactly what I needed. For several months, I had been working long hours on the Unilever account. I had given notice at the agency and I was working on my final project before joining 4.0, a new digital agency making waves on Madison Avenue. As the newly appointed creative director, I would not have direct responsibility for new business, but I knew the importance of securing an early win when coming in from the outside. I also knew the Unilever account was up for review come September, so I stayed close to all the right people and worked night and day to ensure a successful campaign launch. It was a double-edged sword, of course; if the campaign were a success, why would Unilever opt for a new agency? I was going to be that reason.

I agreed to start my new position the day after Bode's first day of first grade. I wanted to be home for his first day of school, for his first walk to the bus stop, and, most importantly, when he returned home. With a campaign launch scheduled for mid-July, my plan was to wrap up the Unilever project, empty my office, and spend a solid month with Bode. Things worked to plan, and we were packed and on the road the second week of August.

We agreed to call the cannonball competition a draw and headed back to the room to rinse off before bed. I was exhausted, but Bode insisted on a little bedtime reading. I read to him almost every night before bed, but I quickly grew tired of the classics. After committing the brown bears, hello moons, and hungry caterpillars to memory, I decided it was time to start seeking out more thought-provoking and insightful books. If I had to read one more story about Thomas, Percy, and Sir Topham Hat, I was going to lose it. I shared our quest for more thoughtful books with a friend who happened across a book called *Buddha at Bedtime* and sent it to Bode as a gift. The book is comprised of various retellings of classic Buddhism stories, each emphasizing a different quality like honesty, integrity, peace, compassion and mindfulness. It instantly became our favorite. After each tale, we would review the moral, and I'd have Bode repeat it to me in his own words. No matter how sleepy he appeared, he always grasped the lesson straight away. I'd often wonder at how incredibly his mind worked, effortlessly absorbing new information and life lessons.

We read the final story in the book—for the third time— back in New Orleans, so I suggested reading the book's introduction about who the Buddha was and what Buddhism is about. I had read the introduction to him once, about a year ago, but because it seemed a bit advanced for him at the time, we skipped it the next two times through the book. Bode agreed to have me start with the introduction, but by the time I got through the part about who the Buddha was, he was sound asleep.

The next morning, we enjoyed a breakfast buffet on the restaurant's patio. The view was unusual with the tall buildings of downtown San Diego providing the backdrop—beyond the water—rather than the vast ocean and endless blue sky that I typically associate with a waterfront hotel. It was only three or four hours to Punta Cabras, so I was in no rush to abandon the comfort of our hotel. After breakfast, we made our way to the pool, and I sat on a lounge chair while Bode sat atop the hotel wall facing the bay. With Bode in my line-of-sight, I opened the *New York Times* app on my phone and caught up on the world news I had successfully avoided for the past week: the market was at an all-time high; the Yankees were on a twelve-game losing streak, their longest since 1913; Tibetan monks had still not discovered the reincarnation of the 14th Dalai Lama, and China was threatening to appoint its own amidst protests; Elon Musk unveiled a new space capsule; mega-celebs Christian Bates and Emily Anderson were spotted holding hands in Beverly Hills. I tapped on the article about Tibet.

After a few minutes of reading, something blocked the sun, and I looked up to see Bode standing on the wall performing sun salutations. Naja had told me he had taken a liking to yoga, but I had never seen him practice. His movements were so smooth, so natural, and I was in awe of his poise and balance. I wondered how long he had been doing this. It reminded me to check in with Naja before crossing the border so I sent her a quick text. *All ok? Crossing border in an hour or so. Hope you're enjoying your holiday! How long has B been practicing yoga?!?*

Her response was swift: *Incredible, isn't he? Lol . . . my little yogi! Give him a million kisses 4 me! Have fun & be safe!*

I had been to maybe twenty or thirty yoga classes since moving to Connecticut, but I was nothing like Bode. He was incredible, his movements fluid, his postures completely aligned. He moved with such grace, such ease. He looked like one of the instructors at the yoga studio in Westport. How long has he been practicing? *Was this normal?* I nearly dropped the phone when Bode faced the bay and performed tree pose on the top of the wall—his right knee bent with his right foot against his left thigh, palms pressed together in prayer before stretching his arms high and wide above his head. It was one of my most challenging poses but Bode balanced effortlessly, not the slightest undulation despite the breeze coming off the water. After about twenty seconds, he brought his hands back through heart center and down by his side. He switched legs, hands in prayer, arms extended. Again, perfectly balanced.

I was astonished. I snapped a photo and then tapped on Naja's name.

"Hi!" she said, "How's it going?"

"Are you kidding me?"

"He's pretty incredible, huh?"

"Naja, he's standing on a friggin wall facing the San Diego Bay with the wind gusting in his face . . . doing tree pose!"

"I know, he's incredible. I want to take him to classes."

"Does he want to go?" I asked.

"I don't know, he usually just shrugs."

"Well, let's sign him up. Kaia Yoga's got kid classes every

week. Have you been going?"

"I usually just practice in the family room. More so lately because Bode's been joining me."

"Well, sign him up at Kaia. See if they have a family membership or something and you guys can go whenever you want."

"Okay, I'll ask him when you guys get home. Where are you now?"

"We're at the Marriott in Coronado. We just ate breakfast, and we're going to hit the road soon."

"How was New Orleans? Did you have breakfast at Slim Goodies?"

"We did, it was amazing. Good recommendation. Did you get our text?"

"Yes, he was so cute!"

"I know. I actually got him to pose for once. I think I'm driving him crazy with all the photos."

"He'll appreciate it one day."

"Hope so. Okay, I'm going to run before he starts doing some inversions on the wall. Everything good with you? Do you need anything?"

She said she was fine, we said our goodbyes, and I hung up. Bode sat on the wall facing me, expressionless.

"How long have you been practicing yoga?" I called to him. I snapped another photo of him with downtown San Diego in the background.

"I don't know." He shrugged. "We did it at school once or twice, but I do it with Naja at home."

"Yeah, she just told me. I told her to sign you up for classes if you want. You're pretty incredible at it."

He flashed a quick smile, hopped off the wall, and sat on the lounge chair beside me. "When are we leaving?"

"In a sec. I just want to finish this article about the Dalai Lama. There's crazy stuff going on in China."

"What's happening?" he asked.

"China is threatening to appoint the next Dalai Lama, and the Tibetans are up in arms."

He looked confused.

"I'll explain in a sec," I said and pulled his shaggy head close to kiss his forehead.

"Where is China?"

"About ten thousand miles that way." I pointed with my thumb over my head. Near where Naja is from, but north."

"Like Canada?"

"Like Canada for us, yes. China is north of Thailand."

"Can we go?" he asked, as usual.

"One day," I said. "Absolutely."

five

"WHO IS THE DALAI LAMA?" Bode asked as we crossed back over the Coronado Bridge.

"The Dalai Lama is the spiritual leader of Tibetan Buddhism," I said. "He died five years ago."

"Five years ago? Why is it crazy in China now then?" he asked, surprising me by connecting the turmoil in China to the Dalai Lama's death.

There had many been many occasions in which Bode would ask an intelligent question that presented a common parental dilemma: answer it truthfully or sugarcoat it for little ears? Early on, I decided to be as honest as possible with Bode, no matter how age-inappropriate others may regard the subject matter. I figured that if he was bright enough or mature enough to ask a question, he was entitled to an honest answer. Of course, things would get tricky from time to time when he would ask about things such as his mother and the circumstances surrounding her death. As often as possible, I would answer Bode's questions as if he were my contemporary, never speaking down to him. He wasn't shy about asking questions, that's for sure, and I often found myself looking forward to his next one. Each time I considered sugarcoating an answer, I'd recall how well he had understood the previous explanation. I also considered all the things he wouldn't have learned if I held back information I thought was too mature for him.

I looked into the rearview and saw that Bode was waiting for an answer. "Well, the article said that Tibet's high priests haven't found the Dalai Lama's reincarnation yet, and China is threatening to appoint their own against the wishes of the Tibetan people."

"Can they do that?"

"I'm not sure," I said.

"What does the article say?"

"It says that for the past five hundred years, the Dalai Lama had been selected by Tibetan monks. Buddhist monks, led by a high priest called the Panchen Lama, would search for his reincarnation after his death. It took them four years to find the 14th Dalai Lama."

Bode still seemed interested, so I continued.

"There's been tension between China and Tibet for years, increasingly so as the Dalai Lama aged. When he died in 2017, it marked the first death of a Dalai Lama since China took control of Tibet. And now, China is threatening to appoint the new one by choosing the name of a high priest from an urn."

A few seconds passed.

"Dad?"

"Yeah, buddy?"

"How could the next Dalai Lama be a high priest if the last one died five years ago? Shouldn't it be a kid?"

"That's a great question," I said, impressed that he came to such a conclusion. "I guess so."

A minute passed and then Bode asked, "So, what's going to happen now?"

"I'm not sure. The article talks about two Panchen Lamas— one appointed by the 14th Dalai Lama and one appointed by the

Chinese government." I stopped—perhaps abruptly—not feeling up to the task of explaining the apparent abduction of the Panchen Lama who was appointed by the Dalai Lama in 1995. As the article stated, many Tibetans feared that the six-year-old Panchen Lama and his family were kidnapped, and likely assassinated, by Chinese authorities. In any event, no one had seen or heard from the boy since, which was unfortunate considering his destined role to help identify the next Dalai Lama.

Fortunately, Bode steered the conversation back to the Dalai Lama by asking what he did exactly.

"Like I said, he's the spiritual leader of Tibetan Buddhism. He is believed to be an incarnation of the Buddha of Compassion."

Crickets.

"You there?"

"Yeah. I'm just thinking. Why does he reincarnate?"

"Well, Buddhists believe that *all* living beings reincarnate, right?"

"Like Mom and Sophie."

"Exactly," I said, looking up to the rearview. "But the Buddha of Compassion *chooses* to reincarnate, rather than become a Buddha, so he can teach others how to end suffering. He is what's called a *bodhisattva*. That's what the original Buddha called himself before he became enlightened."

"The Buddha that we read about last night."

"I thought you fell asleep," I said.

"No, I was awake."

I smiled at him in the rearview. "If you want, we can read more about him tonight. Or tomorrow depending on how we feel after setting up camp. It introduces Buddhism a whole lot better than I can. Jorge is into this stuff, too, and he'll probably know more about what's going on in China."

"Okay," he said and turned to look out the window. "How far 'til Mexico?"

"*Un*til. Finish your words," I said, sounding very much like my father. "We'll be at the border in about ten minutes."

"Really?" he said, sitting up high on his booster seat in a rare display of excitement. He had never left the country and was clearly pumped to begin his life as a world traveler. The word *wanderlust* came to mind. It was one of my favorites and perhaps it ran in the family.

"Are you excited to meet Jorge?" I asked.

"Yep."

"Can you say *hola?*"

"*Hola.*"

"That means 'hello.'"

"*Hola*!" he repeated.

"*Cómo estás*? That means 'How are you."

"*Cómo estás*?"

"Put it together. Say 'Hello, how are you?'"

"*Hola, cómo estás*?"

"Good job! Okay, one more. Jorge's last name is Espinoza. Can you say, *mucho gusto, Señor Espinoza*?"

"*Mucho gusto, Señor Epsinoza.*"

"Close. It's Espinoza, not Epsinoza. Say Espinoza."

"Epsinoza."

"Close enough. You've got three hours to practice," I said. "Look there, international border, five hundred feet. You excited?"

"Yep," he said, still sitting at attention.

I slowed the truck to twenty-five miles per hour and entered one of the lanes that read, *Nada que declare*, and stopped at the red mini traffic light.

"What'd that say?" Bode asked, gesturing toward the blue sign overhead with his chin.

"*Nada que declare*. Nothing to declare," I said, intrigued how Bode distinguished Spanish from English, considering he couldn't read yet.

The red light turned green, and just as I lifted my foot from the brake, a thunderous voice shouted, "Stop!" I covered the brake and awaited further direction. Typically, no questions are asked as you enter Mexico, and I was surprised to be stopped. What I took to be a Mexican border patrol agent dressed in a light green, short-sleeved button-down and dark green trousers approached and asked me in English where we were headed.

"Camping near Eréndira."

"Would you please step out of the vehicle?"

"No, not here," I said.

"Sir?"

"I'm not stepping out of the vehicle with my son in the back."

He smiled. "Of course. Kindly pull over to the side, and I will be over in a minute."

"Is there a problem, *Señor . . . Gutierrez*?" I asked, saying the vowels slowly in an attempt to not mangle his name.

"Kindly pull to the side, and I will be over in a minute." He mumbled some Spanish into a radio that he held close to his mouth.

I wasn't about to start an argument at the border, so I pulled the car up about fifty feet and to the right.

"What's wrong, Dad?"

"I'm not sure. Sit tight, okay?"

I killed the engine and stared at my side mirror. Gutierrez was speaking with another border patrol officer wearing a similar uniform but in shades of blue. American, I thought. Gutierrez shrugged, and the two men approached our truck.

"Good morning, sir. My name is Officer Rodriguez with U.S. Border Patrol," the man in blue said. "Would you please step out of the vehicle?"

I removed the key from the ignition and told Bode to hang tight. Officer Rodriguez guided the door open for me, and I stepped out of the truck. I tucked the keys in my pocket and said, "Is there something wrong? Do you need to see my passport?"

"Sir, who is the boy in the vehicle?" Rodriguez asked as he walked me to the back of the truck. Gutierrez removed his cap and wiped the sweat from his brow with a forearm.

"My son," I said. "Why?"

"Do you have papers?"

"Of course." If there was one thing I made sure of as a single dad, it was to always have a copy of Bode's papers with me. The world has changed so much since I was a kid and everyone was always asking to see Bode's papers. As a parent, I guess I should be happy that people took extra precaution, but it was frustrating when they doubted me, one of the good guys. I walked to the passenger side and opened the door. The seat was pulled up to give Bode legroom, so I sat sideways with my legs out the door and opened the glove box. I pulled out the 6 x 9 envelope labeled *Bode* and told Bode I'd be right back. The officers were waiting for me on the side of the truck now. I removed the copies of Bode's birth certificate and social security card.

"Son, will you please step out of the vehicle?"

Bode looked at me and I nodded. He unbuckled his seatbelt and climbed out.

"What is your name, son?" Officer Rodriguez asked.

"Bode."

"What's your last name?"

"Price."

"Why does it say Hubert here?" Rodriguez asked.

"Because that's his given name. Bode is his middle name," I said.

Rodriguez's finger scanned the document, and it stopped on Bode's middle name.

"It's pronounced Boh-dee," I said. "It's what he goes by."

Rodriguez looked over at Bode and asked, "How old are you, son?"

"Five and three quarters," Bode replied proudly.

"What's with his eyes?" Gutierrez asked.

"Excuse me?" I said.

"His eyes. Why are they different colors?"

"Seriously?" I asked. "Those are his eyes."

"*Rodriguez, miro esto.*"

Officer Rodriguez removed his sunglasses and took a closer look at Bode. "Interesting," he said. He put his shades back on. "Office Gutierrez says you are headed to Eréndira. That's not a very well-known town. What brings you there?"

"There's a surf spot a few miles up the coast," I said. "I used to surf there back in college."

Rodriguez glanced up at the surfboard strapped to roof of the Land Cruiser. "Where are you staying?"

"We're camping."

Gutierrez shaded the sun with two hands as he peered into the truck's back window. Rodriguez handed me the documents. "One more thing," he said.

"Yes?"

"Where is the boy's mother?"

I was hoping he wouldn't ask that in front of Bode.

"She's dead," Bode said.

Rodriguez looked down at Bode.

"She died when I was born," Bode said.

Rodriguez looked back at me and I nodded. "I'm sorry. And I'm sorry for delaying you. Please enjoy your visit." He made eye contact with Gutierrez and dismissed him with a jerk the head.

Gutierrez nodded apologetically and walked away.

"You have enough gas until Ensenada?" Rodriguez asked, which I took as a recommendation to not make any stops before Ensenada.

"I do, thank you," I said.

"Safe travels," he said and walked away.

I turned to Bode. "Hop in, buddy. Let's get out of here."

I started the truck and merged back onto the highway. Within seconds, we were surrounded by the traffic, noise and intensity of Tijuana. Instantly, everything became gray, as if the sun itself was frightened of crossing the border and hid behind the clouds. There was a certain heaviness in the air that made it difficult to breathe. I closed the windows and flipped on the A/C. We crossed a bridge and followed the curve of the road to the left. I glanced in the rearview to see Bode taking it all in, his mouth open in what I assumed was disbelief at all the external stimuli. We were nearly a mile from the border, and I couldn't help but notice the backlog of bumper-to-bumper traffic in the opposite direction, crawling toward the United States.

Throughout my time at USC, I had been the primary driver for our treks to Baja. Besides being one of only a few of my friends to own a car, I was blessed with an excellent sense of direction. I don't recall having a GPS back then, yet I always seemed to know which way was north. Often, if we took a buddy's car, I would drive the leg between San Diego and Ensenada. The directions through the labyrinths of Tijuana and Ensenada seemed etched in my muscles and I could have made the drive blind. The problem was that I wasn't blind, and many of my visual landmarks often changed: pharmacies would no longer be in business and were replaced with office supply stores or minimarts, rundown buildings would be under construction with scaffolding blocking signs and other landmarks, gas stations became empty lots, even a McDonald's had moved. The most confusing part was the sheer number of banks, all with similar names: Banco Banorte, Banco Bajanorte, Banco Santander, Banco HSBC, Banco Banamex, Banco Banamer, and so on.

I turned right before the second roundabout at Banco Banorte and took the shortcut to Mexico 1. Though technically it was the main highway, it was several miles before we escaped the congestion of central Tijuana.

"Dad?"

"Hmmm?"

"Was I really born outside?"

"What made you think of that?"

"Nothing," he said, though I assumed it had something to do with Rodriguez's question about his mother.

I eyed him in the rearview. "Well yeah, you were. You don't remember the story?"

He shrugged. "Tell me again."

"Well, I was in the shower the morning your mom went into labor. I heard her shouting but couldn't make out the words. When I rushed into the bedroom, I found her sitting on the floor against the wall, smiling with tears in her eyes. 'He's coming,' is all she said. Your mom had her entire pregnancy planned out, and we were scheduled to go to a birthing center in Danbury. I grabbed her bag and helped her to the truck when all of a sudden she stopped and said, 'We're not going to make it.' It was still early morning, and there wasn't anyone outside. I helped her to the lawn and lowered her to the ground against the maple tree before dialing 911. It was cold outside, real cold, and I'm not sure why she pulled me to the lawn instead of inside. She was breathing fast and hard and kept repeating, 'He's coming, he's coming, he's coming.' I relayed everything to the emergency operator who kept telling me to remain calm though I was anything but; your mom was always the calm one."

I looked up to see if Bode was still listening. He was.

"A policeman arrived in just a few minutes with an ambulance right behind. By the time the EMT got to her, your little head was in my hands. I was so scared, buddy, you have no idea. There was no way to move Mom into the ambulance so they delivered you right on the lawn. Immediately after you were born, they loaded us into the back of the ambulance and took us to the hospital. I held you tight the entire time, wrapped in these tiny little blankets. You were absolutely perfect. Except for those funny eyes, at least."

"You're teasing."

"Yes, I'm teasing. You were perfect. You're still perfect."

"What about Mommy?"

"Mom was okay. She was exhausted but otherwise she was fine."

"She died in the hospital?"

I had told this story to Bode before, but for some reason he thought that his mom died when he was born. A sudden feeling came over me, a memory about some kid whose mother died during childbirth. Did I see it on TV or read an article? The kid grew up obsessed with guilt that he somehow killed his mother during birth. I tried to shake it out of my head.

"No, buddy, of course not. She was fine. In fact, she came home with you a day later."

I considered sharing the full story then, about how the oncologist ran some tests and concluded that her treatment—which had been delayed for months—would be in vain. How the tumor had penetrated into deeper tissues beyond her cervix. And how the symptoms of pregnancy had masked the symptoms of the tumor spreading to her pelvis, kidneys and beyond. I wanted to tell Bode the whole truth, but I felt the full story might be interpreted just as badly as the notion of her dying as a result of childbirth. At the end of the day, Bode would know the truth: how his mom chose him over her treatment.

"No, she came home with you," I repeated. "She held you every minute of every day the entire week. On her last day, she handed you to me. She was so happy, Bode. I wish you could have known her. She was certain that she'd fulfilled her life's purpose, and she told me so before she died."

"What'd she say?"

"She took my hand and she pulled me close. She said, 'I knew what I was doing. I did it with purpose. Now it's up to him.' And then she went to sleep."

"Up to me? What's up to me?"

"I don't know, buddy." I had pondered that same question for years and was still no closer to figuring it out. Her words, spoken softly and deliberately just moments before her death sounded more like prophecy than anything else. But where would such a profound statement have come from? Needless to say, I didn't sleep much those next few weeks. I would lie awake at night in between feedings and hear her voice over and over again: *Now it's up to him.*

"All I know," I continued, "is that your mom was very determined to bring you into this world."

six

WE DROVE THE REST of the way to Ensenada in near silence, stopping only for tolls and the random police checkpoint inspecting for drugs and guns. I considered stopping in Puerto Nuevo for a lobster lunch but thought better of it, heeding Officer Rodriguez's unspoken advice. It was around midday when we arrived at the Pemex station in Ensenada to refuel and stock up on snacks for the final stretch to Punta Cabras. I had Bode wait in the car while I pumped gas and then the two of us went into the AmPm to do our business and grab some snacks.

Once back on the highway, Bode fired up *E.T.* I was pleased that I was able to identify the scene: Elliott luring E.T. into his bedroom with a trail of Reese's Pieces.

South of Ensenada, the landscape took on the colors of the desert. We quickly found ourselves nestled among mountains of varying heights, cacti, and other low-lying shrubs. The sun finally reappeared and the temperature climbed into the seventies. I opened the sunroof and windows, set the cruise control to sixty, and adjusted my seat to get comfortable.

With Bode watching *E.T.* on the phone, I turned on the CD player. The CD that was in the player was Sigur Ros' *Takk* album. I once read a review on iTunes that said if Planet Earth were ever to broadcast music to the rest of the universe in an effort to make contact with extraterrestrial life, it should be the ethereal melodies of Sigur Ros. As if such an exalted recommendation wasn't enough, I found a number of similar reviews of their *Takk* album before I purchased it: "*You can find evidence in God,*" "*Absolutely magical,*" "*What your memories, compassion, inner peace, and love would sound like if rolled into music,*" and so on.

I was completely at peace, hypnotized by the gentle vibration of the tires against pavement and aurally massaged by the euphonious tunes of *Sæglópur* when all of a sudden four masked gunmen rushed the highway, two from either side, and pointed large, black weapons at the windshield. I brought the truck to a screeching halt and raised my hands up above my shoulders. "Stay calm and don't say a word," I whispered to Bode.

Each of the men had a handkerchief covering their face just below the eyes. One of them approached my door and looked into the truck. With my hands shaking and my shoulders and arms fatigued, I stole a glance in the rearview. Bode sat motionless and—incredibly—expressionless.

"*¿A dónde vas?*" the gunman asked.

"*Eréndira.*"

"*¿Quién es este?*"

"*Mi hijo,*" I said, unsure if I said son or nephew.

"*¿Dónde está su madre?*"

"She's dead," Bode answered from the backseat.

There are no words to describe the depth and range of emotion I felt at that moment: terror, panic, fear, shock, confusion, and maybe even pride for Bode. I looked at the gunman and nodded, "*Está muerta.*"

The gunman considered this for a moment, his rifle strapped around his shoulder and pointed upward. Clearly, we weren't carrying any drugs. Ransom was certainly a possibility, but with the boy's mother dead, with whom would they begin their negotiations? And the boy, what were they going to do with a little boy in the meantime? Extortion seemed to be his best play. After considering his possible moves, my attention turned to my own. Sadly, I only came up with two: attempt to speed away or let the situation play out. While the latter was beyond frightening, the former was sure to draw their ire at best and their bullets at worst. The gunman spit toward the front wheel of the truck and shouted something to the others. When one of them protested, he barked his orders again with more authority. Appearing dejected, the men in front of the truck stepped aside. The gunman flicked his rifle forward and down toward the ground. "*Larguense.*"

I hesitated for a moment, unsure what he said.

"Go!" he shouted over his shoulder and walked away.

He didn't need to tell me twice (in English), so I hit the gas and took off. In the rearview, I watched the four men gather on the side of the road as they got smaller and smaller. My heart was thumping and my entire body shaking. I sat tall and looked at Bode in the rearview who was sitting calm as day.

"You okay, buddy?"

"Yeah."

"You sure?" I said, although it was clear that I was the one in need of comforting. "What was that back there? How'd you understand—"

"We learn Spanish words in school."

"Yeah, but how'd you . . ." I let my words go; it wasn't important. What mattered was that we were alive and safe and distancing ourselves from the gunmen. My body didn't seem to agree, however, and continued to tremble. I wanted to stop the truck to regain my composure and hug Bode but there was no way I was pulling over. I reached back, grabbed his ankle and held it until my shoulder went numb.

The State Department's travel warnings hadn't even mentioned Baja, the one region I knew to be a hotspot for violence in recent years. Perhaps more disturbing was that most of the travel warnings focused on violence between the drug cartels and the Mexican government, rather than the type of crimes that can be expected by tourists. It was one thing to be an innocent bystander while a drug cartel seizes a tollbooth in a gunfight, but it's something entirely different to be singled out in the middle of the highway with a surfboard on your hood.

My heart rate slowed, and the trembling finally ceased. We drove in silence until we reached the turnoff at kilometer marker seventy-eight. "We're on the homestretch. Only fifteen miles to go," I said, steering onto a paved secondary highway. We passed a farm of some sort on the right and headed southwest toward Eréndira and the Pacific.

The road remained paved as it snaked its way through the mountains. As we approached the first houses on the outskirts of Eréndira, Bode became more attentive and started to point out his observations. Many of the houses were situated right up against the road. Some had front doors while others didn't. We saw more than one house with its front door off its hinges and resting against the house. Few homes had a car or pickup truck out front and many had broken appliances, storage bins, and car parts situated around the property. A wash bin sat on nearly every lot with a clothesline nearby. Rusted tricycles and soccer balls that had long lost their vinyl patches littered many of the yards.

"If you like it here, we can stay. This would be your school," I joked as we slowly passed over three speed bumps.

"Where's the playground?"

"Not sure," I said. "See that place? They serve awesome *carne asada* burritos."

"That's a restaurant?"

"Sort of. It's a woman's house, but they renovated the front of it to form a little restaurant. You can sit at that table. There's another place coming up on the left with awesome *carnitas*."

"What are those?"

"Pulled pork tacos," I said, to which I got no response and I started to wonder what he was going to eat all week. "All these places have *cheesadillas*, too," I said and watched his smile appear in the rearview. "And bean burritos, which you like, right?"

He nodded, and I felt a little better although I certainly wasn't planning to drive into Eréndira for every meal. It's not that the five miles was far—though the miles were off-road—but the food we could buy or catch ourselves in Punta Cabras was as fresh as you get. Although Bode regarded seafood with the same distaste he did meat and poultry, I had hoped he would eat what we caught ourselves.

"Just like Westport, huh, buddy?"

After passing through the heart of town—all five blocks of it—the houses started to spread out once again. I pulled over at a service station to fill up the tank and let air out of the tires.

"Why are you doing that?" Bode asked from his open window.

"Because the truck is heavy, and if we don't let some air out we might get stuck in the sand."

"What sand?"

"The next few miles along the water are off-road. It's like sand dunes."

I paid the attendant in U.S. dollars and gave him five extra bucks. I was going to need his help filling up the tires, and I wanted him to remember me, not that there was a chance of him forgetting some *gringo* and his little boy driving a late model Toyota Land Cruiser.

"Ready to see Jorge?" I asked as I climbed into the truck.

"*Mucho gusto, Señor Epsinoza.*"

I smiled. "Espinoza."

"Espinoza," he repeated.

"Excellent. Say it all again now."

"*Mucho gusto, Señor Epsinoza.*"

"Ugh."

Bode giggled, and I started the truck.

In less than a quarter mile, we were at the end of the paved road with nothing but the Pacific ahead. The car filled with the aroma of the sea, and we were able to taste the salt. I proceeded onto the graded dirt road and followed its curve to the right. The tires kicked up dirt so I closed the windows and turned on the A/C. In the rearview I saw that Bode's gaze was fixated out the window, mouth agape, as he stared at the Pacific for the very first time.

"What are those shacks over there?" he said.

"People's houses, I think. Probably local fishermen."

We continued down the dirt road for a couple miles until we came to Coyote Cal's. It looked different from the last time I was there. A new deck had been added on the second level, offering a panoramic view of the ocean.

"This is Coyote Cal's, the place I was telling you about earlier. We'll come back in a bit, but let's first go see Jorge," I said. "Imagine the rest of this drive in total darkness and you'll see why Brett and I never found Punta Cabras our first night."

The dirt road gave way to packed sand as we drove the last three miles north to Punta Cabras, where the sand became looser and we found ourselves driving over dunes for the last half-mile. Tire tracks veered in different directions over each undulation and then re-joined one another at the next, forming elongated figure eights. The sensation was similar to skiing over moguls and made me feel like a teenager driving for the first time. We climbed one final hill before allowing the truck to come to rest on its own, rather than brake and bury our tires in the loose sand. We sat facing west, perched high atop the bluff, and watched as a fresh set of waves made its way toward shore beneath a deep blue sky.

seven

JORGE MUST HAVE HEARD our engine from a mile away because he greeted us atop the dunes, a good 300 meters from his house. He startled me as he approached the truck but I quickly recognized him and jumped out of the truck to give him a hug.

"Matthew, *mi hijo*. I am so sorry," he said, referring to Eliza.

"Thanks, Jorge. It's been a long time. We're okay."

"She was such a lovely spirit, Matthew."

"She still is," I said as Bode climbed out of the truck and stood beside me. "It's good to see you, old man. Meet my son. Bode, this is Jorge."

"It is nice to finally meet you," Jorge said, offering a hand to Bode.

"*Mucho gusto, Señor Espinoza,*" he said correctly, and I couldn't help but laugh.

"*Mucho gusto, Señor Bode, mucho gusto.*" Jorge lifted Bode into the air and gave him a hug. "Your dad has told me much about you. But you're not nearly as ugly as he made me believe!"

Bode giggled as Jorge tickled him before putting him down. I walked to the back of the truck and opened the tailgate.

"Look at those eyes," Jorge said. "Beautiful. Have you stolen them from an angel?"

Bode and Jorge joined me at the back of the truck and we began to unload some of our gear. There were two other tents set up and I asked Jorge if he knew the owners.

"Just two couples from Northern California on a road trip to Cabo. They're leaving in the morning but others will be coming for sure. They didn't take your favorite spot, though," gesturing to the flat sand beside the truck.

After emptying most of our gear, we set up our tent and the E-Z Up for the kitchen area. When I pulled the chairs out, I noticed the empty iPad box.

"Hey, Jorge, I brought you something." I opened the driver's side door and reached between the seat and console for the charged tablet.

"What is it? One of those electronic book readers?"

"It's called an iPad. It's a tablet computer. You're going to love it. You can do a lot with it, but most of all you'll be able to call and email Ana and Pablo. You'll even be able to see them while talking."

"Matthew, thank you. I have no idea what this is, but it looks like it cost you a fortune. It was not necessary."

"It's my pleasure, Jorge. Let's bring it to Coyote Cal's, and I'll show you how it works. I've got a bottle of scotch for Rick, too."

We climbed in the truck and drove the three miles back to Coyote Cal's. When we pulled up, Rick was up on the deck and he called down to us.

"Who's that?" he shouted with a feigned accusatory tone.

"It's the *fire-stahta*," I said in my best British accent, trying to sound like The Prodigy in their song, *Firestarter*. Years earlier, I accidentally set fire to the trash outside Coyote Cal's when a Roman candle went awry. Rick had forgiven me long ago, but— like an uncle calls his nephew a troublemaker—he had gotten in the habit of calling me the firestarter, and it stuck.

"Ahh, Mr. Price. It's been a long time. Come, come. Let me

get a look at you."

We climbed the stairs and joined Rick on the deck. He was behind a half moon-shaped tiki bar putting away a rack of pint glasses. I shook Rick's extended hand and presented him with a bottle of Glenfiddich. He accepted it graciously before slamming three shot glasses onto the wood bar. He turned to grab an open bottle from the top shelf, and I flashed a smile to Jorge. Rick poured three overflowing shots and we toasted to old friends.

"Who's this boy?" Rick shouted, slamming his glass to the bar. "Does he drink?"

"This is my son. Bode, this is Rick, but you can call him Coyote Cal."

"Mucho gusto, Señor Coyote Cal."

"Mucho gusto, Bode. Welcome to my little slice of heaven. Can I buy you a drink, young man?"

Bode looked at me and I nodded.

"Pineapple juice?" Bode asked, peering over the bar.

Rick smiled and filled a lowball glass with juice and refilled our shot glasses. "To the little man with jewels for eyes." We clinked glasses and drank.

We moved to a couch on the deck, where I sat between Bode and Jorge. Rick brought over a few bottles of water and provided us the highly secure password to his wireless network: coyotecals. I had already downloaded a few apps after purchasing the device, so I fired up Safari and created an email account for Jorge. We were in the same time zone as Brett in L.A., so I typed in his number and sent him a text: *Yt? I'm in Punta Cabras with Jorge and wanna test Facetime.* Within seconds, Brett replied: *One sec, on phone . . .*

"Is that your friend Brett from USC?" Jorge asked.

"It is. He'll be psyched to see you."

"*See me*? How will he—"

The incoming call flashed on the screen and I accepted Brett's call. Within a few seconds, Brett appeared in perfect clarity from his office in L.A. "Hey, hey," he said. "You're in Punta Cabras?"

"We are! I'm here with Bode. But there's someone here who wants to say hello first." I passed the tablet to Jorge and helped him angle it toward his face so Brett could see him.

"Jorge! How are you? It's been years."

"Hello, my friend. *Cómo está?*" Jorge stammered, perplexed by the technology and why he was talking to a computer and how Brett was able to see him.

"Good, good. It's nice to see you. You've got some visitors. Is Bodeman there, too? Let me see that monster."

Jorge passed the device to Bode who smiled wide for Uncle Brett.

"Hey, buddy! How are you?"

"Good. Hi," Bode said bashfully.

"You're huge, dude. And look at that hair! Tell your dad to get you a haircut. You're a climber, not a surfer."

Bode smiled and buried his face against my arm. I think he was more tired than shy.

"Matt," Brett continued. "You're a maniac, bringing that kid to Mexico. What are you thinking?"

"Don't ask," I said, angling the camera back toward me. "We had a bit of a run-in earlier."

Jorge looked confused because I hadn't yet told him about the drive down.

"I'll tell you about it later," I said to Jorge. "Hey, so, I've got a bunch of things to show Jorge on this thing before sundown so we're gonna run. We'll try to call you tomorrow or over the weekend."

"Sounds good. Good seeing you, Jorge. See ya', Bode. Cut that hair!"

"*Adios, amigo.*" Jorge said, leaning toward the tablet, not yet understanding that he need not speak directly into the microphone.

I tapped the red button to hang up the call and turned to Jorge. "What do you think?"

"*Increíble.*"

"Well, get used to it because you're going to be able to see Ana, Pablo, and us all the time now."

"Matthew, how can I thank you? This is . . . too much."

"Jorge, it's my pleasure. Let me show you more."

We spent an hour browsing the web and checking out some of the apps I had previously downloaded for him—YouTube, ESPN, Pandora. I bookmarked a bunch of websites and showed him how to use Google.

"Want to send your first email?" I pulled out my phone, found Coyote Cal's wireless network, and entered the password.

"Okay, click on that little *new mail* button. I've already added me to your address book so all you need to do is start typing my name and my email address will appear."

Slowly, Jorge pecked the first two letters of my name. My name popped up and he glanced at me before tapping it. I tapped on the *Subject* field and typed *Test*. He then tapped the body of the email and started to hunt and peck: *Hola, Matthew. Thank you for the computer. -Jorge* I pointed to the *Send* button and Jorge tapped it. Within seconds, my phone sounded a chime and I showed him the new mail.

"Congratulations," I said. "You've sent your first email. I hope you never have to send and receive three hundred a day like me."

Jorge looked confused.

"Never mind. What do you say we get out of here? What do you think, big guy? Want to start a fire?"

"Not here!" Rick called from behind the bar.

Bode nodded and rubbed his eyes.

"Looks like Buddha will have to wait until tomorrow night, huh?" I said, knuckling his head. "Hey Jorge, do we need firewood?"

"No, my friend. I have plenty. *Vamos.*"

On the ride back to Punta Cabras, I told Jorge about the gunmen on the highway. Grateful for our well-being, he assured me that it had been much safer in recent years and what we Americans had been hearing from the media was likely blown out of proportion. Most of the violence in Baja, he said, was a result of the drug cartels fighting for control of the trafficking routes into the United States. The violence against tourists had abated in recent years, as evidenced by our safe passage, but the alarming increase in violence between the cartels has overshadowed the progress. Despite Jorge's encouraging words regarding the improving conditions for tourists, I was still disconcerted and not looking forward to the drive north. After all, having masked gunmen rush your vehicle—intentionally or not—hardly felt like progress in a historically peaceful locale.

We finished setting up camp as the sun began its descent. I set up two retractable tables beneath the E-Z Up and laid out two bins full of kitchen items and miscellaneous gear while Bode unpacked the sleeping bags. Jorge returned with his truck and unloaded a bundle of wood.

"That should hold you through breakfast," he said. "I have plenty more back at the house."

"Thank you," I said. "Are you guys hungry?"

Bode nodded and Jorge shrugged as he knelt down to prepare the fire pit. Bode watched attentively from his beach chair and Jorge called him over to help. While they tended to the fire, I rummaged through our cooler to see what was left in the icy water. I found a few wraps that I had forgotten about and took them out to thaw. I cracked open a couple Pacificos and handed one to Jorge and a juice box to Bode.

We sat quietly as the sun took its evening dip into the ocean. Brilliant shades of yellow fought nobly to hold off the oranges, heedless of the reds that crept in while their backs were turned. Colors twisted and blended and overtook one another as the sky labored to create a flawless imitation of an Albert Bierstadt masterpiece.

I tossed Bode the vegetarian wrap and offered half the turkey and avocado wrap to Jorge, who waved it away. How he managed to live on such little sustenance was beyond me. I held out a bag of Russet potato chips, and he grabbed a handful. I poured a pile onto Bode's paper plate and then my own and kicked back to watch the final act of the sunset as the waves crashed below.

"Tell me about Buddha," Jorge said, reaching for more chips.

"What do you mean?" I asked.

"Earlier at Coyote Cal's, you told Bode that Buddha will have to wait until tomorrow."

I took a sip of my beer. "We've got a book called *Buddha at Bedtime*. It's a bunch of stories based on traditional Buddhist tales. The other night we started reading the introduction again about who the Buddha was—"

"Last night," Bode corrected.

"Was that last night? You're right. It's been a long day. Anyway, we're up to the part that introduces Buddhism."

"Are you interested in Buddhism, *muchacho*?"

Bode nodded, and I ran my fingers through his hair.

"We do need to chop this, buddy. Hey Jorge, earlier today I was telling Bode about an article in *The New York Times* about what's going on in China. He asked me why China invaded Tibet. Do you know what happened? It was before I was born."

"It happened before I was born, too," Jorge said with a smile. "Several years before, actually, in 1950." He cleared his throat. "China defeated the Tibetan army in just two weeks and sent a captured Tibetan commander to Lhasa, Tibet's capital, with the terms for negotiation. The Tibetan government later signed something called the 'Seventeen Point Agreement' that granted Tibet some autonomy but essentially allowed China to rule Tibet."

"Why would they do that?" Bode asked.

"They didn't have much of a choice."

Bode considered this for a moment and then asked, "Then what happened?"

"Well, a few years later, China started imposing reforms—"

"What does that mean?" Bode asked.

"They started making changes in Tibet," I said.

"Yes, so, as the Chinese started to implement social and land reform, rebellions erupted once again. When the fighting reached Lhasa in 1959, the Dalai Lama fled to Dharamsala, India. It's where the Tibetan government operates to this day."

I couldn't tell if Bode was confused or just taking it all in. Knowing him, probably the latter.

"The struggle of the Tibetans continued for many years. In 1960, China was accused of cultural genocide after years of massacres, tortures and killings. Monasteries were destroyed, and entire villages were wiped out. I thought things were finally going to get better in the Eighties when the region started to receive international attention, especially in the U.S., but nothing really improved. Tibet is still controlled by China, and the Tibetan government is still in exile. Sadly, I have a feeling it's about to get worse, especially if the Tibetans discover the reincarnation of Dalai Lama before China appoints one."

Bode stood and put another log on the fire. He then walked over and climbed onto my lap. I pulled him up so his head rested below my chin and kissed him on the head. "I know, buddy," I said and hugged him close.

Jorge sensed Bode's sadness and changed the subject. "Your dad tells me you like to hike. Would you boys like to explore the foothills tomorrow?" Jorge motioned with his beer over my head but darkness had already fallen.

Bode nodded and turned his head so his cheek was against me.

"You tired, handsome?"

He nodded.

"It's still pretty early. Want to read a story and go to sleep?"

I couldn't tell if his response was a no or just a cozying up.

"Why don't we get you to bed?" I suggested.

"Will you come, too?"

"We'll call it an early night tonight. We've had a long day."

Jorge gave a smile and stood up. He grabbed our empties with one hand and placed his other on Bode's head. "*Mucho gusto*, Bode. I enjoyed meeting you, *muchacho*. I'll see you boys tomorrow." With that, Jorge gave my shoulder a squeeze and walked into the darkness. We listened to the sound of his truck as he drove slowly toward his house.

I sat for a few minutes longer, staring at the fire and listening to the crackling of the wood. I wondered how Jorge knew so much about China and the plight of the Tibetans. To my knowledge, Jorge never received a formal education, but he always seemed to know a lot about things in life that actually mattered. Bode's eyes were closed, and he was resting peacefully against my chest. I stood up with his limp body in my arms and kicked a couple of the logs off the top of the fire. I walked over the E-Z Up and slipped my hand into one of the bins to feel around for my knife. I grabbed my headlamp from the table and made my way into the tent. Bode knew to close the zippers to keep bugs out, but that made it challenging for me to get us inside without waking him up. Once inside, the light from the dying fire barely penetrated the tent, so I flipped on my headlamp and zipped Bode into his sleeping bag. I kissed him on the forehead, turned off the light, and slipped into my bag. After getting cozy, I watched Bode's silhouette as he breathed softly, his neck lit by the flickering light of the dying fire. He appeared to be sleeping comfortably, so I closed my eyes and rolled over.

"Dad?"

"Yeah, buddy," I said over my shoulder.

"I gotta pee."

eight

I WOKE TO A BRIGHTLY lit tent seemingly minutes after I had finally fallen asleep. I had never slept well in tents no matter how soft the ground or how many pillows I surrounded myself with. Any true camper will agree that pillows are cheating, but if I'm not trekking it on foot and there is space for a pillow or two in the truck, I'm bringing them.

My ability to estimate the time of day goes out the window once I zip myself into a tent. I always feel like it's later than it is. I think I finally got to sleep around four though it was probably more like twelve or one. Although I tossed and turned much of the night, I slept soundly the last few hours before daybreak and felt well-rested. I figured it was about nine when I turned to Bode, but he was gone. Normally, I wouldn't think anything of it, but it was our first night in Baja, and I was still skittish after our highway encounter.

I called his name but got no response. I pulled open the zipper and crawled out of the tent. "Bode?" I did a three-sixty but the sand dunes only afforded me a view thirty yards or so in each direction. I looked away from the shore in the direction of Jorge's house, but all I could see were acres of desert. I took a few steps toward the bluff and looked at the ocean. Just as my heart began its ascent into my throat, I caught sight of him down below. He was meditating and couldn't hear me over the crashing waves.

Relieved, I let him be and went to brush my teeth and set out the pans for breakfast. I brewed a pot of coffee and grabbed our duffle bag from the car.

I sat with my coffee facing the ocean when I saw a little head pop up over the bluff. Bode climbed up the steepest portion instead of just walking twenty feet to the path between the dunes.

"Hi," he said.

"Good morning."

He gave me a big hug.

"Thank you. You scared me this morning."

"Why?"

"Because you were gone when I woke up and I couldn't find you."

"I was right there."

"Yes, but I couldn't see you. And you didn't hear me calling."

"You were calling me?" he asked.

"I was, but you couldn't hear me over the ocean."

"Sorry."

"It's okay. Do you know the time?"

"No."

"Where's the phone?" I asked myself, as I patted the pockets of my cargo shorts. I pulled out the phone. "7:26."

"That's it? I thought it was like nine or something," he said.

I smiled. "Me, too. You want breakfast? We have eggs, granola bars, cereal—"

"Do you have tortillas? I'll have a *cheesadilla*."

"Will you?" I smiled. "Yes, I have lots of tortillas. I'll make you one," I said before considering how I was going to manage that without an oven or microwave.

I prepared breakfast for Bode while he brushed his teeth and changed out of yesterday's clothing. I cracked two eggs into a bowl and turned in the direction of Jorge's house to see if he was going to join us. It was several hundred meters away, but the land was flat, and you could have easily spotted a person walking among the low-lying shrubs. There was no sign of him or his truck, so I returned the egg carton to the cooler. I fried up some bacon and used the grease for the eggs. I set my plate on the cooler and dragged it close to our chairs.

"What do you want to do today?" I asked.

"Jorge said we can take a hike into the foothills."

"We can do that. I don't see his truck, but we'll see if he's up for it when he returns. Want to learn to surf this morning?"

"Maybe," he said apprehensively.

It's funny what we become fearful of and how most fears are irrational, based upon possibilities that never occur. While I was terrified of sailing, I had no problem surfing. I capsized a sailboat back in summer camp, but I don't recall feeling afraid. Perhaps I never considered the lake deep enough to drown in, though that didn't make sense. A more likely explanation for my phobia, considering my inclination for surfing, was the absence of a shoreline. After all, it wasn't until Eliza and I went sailing well out into the ocean that my fear surfaced. It was the speed mostly, and how it always seemed faster when I looked down at the water. I remember white-knuckling the side of the boat as Eliza gracefully tacked and jibed, adjusted the sheet, and maneuvered the tiller. I couldn't understand how we could sail so fast and not be tossed overboard. It felt like holding onto the back of a friend's bicycle while skateboarding. You would scream, "Faster, faster," until you reached a point where the skateboard would wobble uncontrollably and you wiped out in the street. It was inevitable, but that was the point of the game—see how fast you can go before the skateboard flies out. Sailing provided the same sensation but for some reason, the boat never capsized with Eliza at the helm. I wouldn't have a clue as to what she was doing so I concentrated my efforts on Eliza's two simple directions: don't make sudden movements that would shift the weight of the boat; and don't let the boom hit me in the head. Needless to say, I only mastered one of her directives. Eliza would smile behind dark sunglasses, as she navigated us through tempestuous winds at frightening speeds. My all-time favorite photograph of her was taken from this vantage point while sailing on our honeymoon in the Caribbean. I remember releasing my grip from the boat just long enough to take the photo. Right as I snapped the picture, she lifted her arm to comb back a lock of hair from her face. My initial thought was that her arm blocked her face, but after having the pictures developed, I was surprised to see that the photo was perfect. She was smiling and her arm framed her bronzed face. The sun was shining on her, and you could see both her eyes through the lenses of her shades. Freckles that only appeared when her skin was tan were visible on her cheeks. I had the photo framed twice: one for the desk in my office and one blown up in black and white for the entertainment center at home.

"Maybe?" I repeated. "Are you afraid?"

"No, I just don't know how to do it."

"Well, I'll show you, monkey," I said. "We won't go deep and you can take your time."

"Okay."

Jorge pulled up while I was cleaning the dishes and utensils from breakfast. He asked if we were still interested in taking a hike into the mountains, and we said we were. He kicked back in one of the chairs while Bode and I put on our shoes and filled our CamelBaks.

Bella was in the flatbed and before we all climbed in, Jorge opened the tailgate to allow her to hop out and meet Bode and smell me for the first time in years. She cried with delight as Bode petted her head and gave her a few scratches behind the ears. It was the first time I had seen Bode pay real attention to any dog since Sophie died. Bella performed multiple three-sixties and galloped back and forth between us, recalling my scent, getting an affirmative pat on the rump, and then scampering back to Bode for more attention.

"I haven't seen her move like that in months," Jorge said.

"She's still so beautiful, Jorge. A little white around the muzzle, but who am I to talk?" I scratched the grays on the side of my head. "Oh, before I forget . . . we brought her some stuff, too."

"Matthew—"

I opened the tailgate to the truck and pulled out two 30-pound bags of food, some treats and bones. I loaded it all into the back of Jorge's truck.

"Matthew, that was unnecessary. Thank you."

"It's nothing. You guys ready?"

I lifted Bella, who was hesitating behind Jorge's pickup, and placed her in the back. The three of us climbed into the cab and headed over to his house so he could leave the truck and Bella behind. I watched as Bode's mouth slowly opened, as we approached the house that Jorge built more than twenty years ago.

"You *live* here?" he asked.

"*Si, mi casa,*" Jorge replied. "Come, let me show you around."

Jorge opened the tailgate for Bella and I followed him to the house. We stopped in the doorway when we noticed Bode hadn't followed. We turned back to see him inspecting a cage of some sort out front.

"What do you have in there?" I asked Jorge.

"Just a couple *crótalos*. Rattlesnakes. We'll release them on the mountain."

We watched as Bode kneeled down for a closer inspection. One of the snakes slowly rose to attention and gave a jab at the side of the cage. It would have sent me head over heels, but surprisingly Bode didn't flinch. He just kneeled there, staring into the cage.

"C'mon, buddy."

"Why do you keep them in a cage?" Bode asked, frowning as he walked into the house.

"So they don't bite me or Bella," Jorge laughed. "We'll take them with us to the mountain and let them go there."

"Oh," Bode said, looking relieved.

Jorge's house was only a few rooms. Two of the rooms were completely empty, and there wasn't much in the way of furniture or decoration. "I love what you've done in here, Jorge," I joked.

We laughed as Bode looked around wide-eyed. "You don't have a kitchen?"

"You're standing in it," Jorge replied. "No electricity, so it's simple."

Bode looked at the statue above the mantle. Jorge picked it up and handed it to him.

"Do you know who that it is?" Jorge asked.

Bode shook his head.

"Isn't that Buddha?" I asked.

"Actually, he's called Budai, though many Westerners call him the Laughing Buddha."

"He looks different from the one in the book," Bode observed, referring to Shakyamuni Buddha, the original Buddha depicted in his storybook.

"There are many different interpretations of what the original Buddha looked liked," Jorge said. "A lot of Westerners believe this is him because folklore has spread to the West quicker than Buddhist religion."

"Huh," I said to myself, one of those mistaken Westerners.

"The Laughing Buddha is not actually considered a Buddha by many Buddhists. Budai is a Chinese folkloric deity. His name means *cloth sack* because of the bag he carries, holding his few possessions. He is admired for his happiness and wisdom of contentment despite having very little."

"What's the deal with rubbing his big belly, Jorge?" I asked.

"Yes, a lot of people think that rubbing his belly will bring good luck, wealth and prosperity, though I always felt that was contradictory to what he symbolizes—contentment with less."

"So, was he a Buddha?" Bode asked, rubbing the belly with two fingers.

"Some say yes, some say no. Some believe he was a *bodhisattva* called Maitreya, the future Buddha."

"The original Buddha didn't look like this one, did he?"

"Shakyamuni Buddha is often represented as tall, lean and good looking," Jorge said. "Of course, there are no photographs of the original Buddha, so who really knows?"

Bode handed the bronze statue back to Jorge who placed it back on the mantle. Finished with the tour, we walked back outside. Bella was lying outside the front door beside a La-Z-Boy.

"She looks comfortable."

"It's our favorite spot," Jorge said. "Shall we?"

Bode and I nodded and Bode shouted, "*Vamos!*"

Jorge picked up the rattlesnake cage by its handle, and we walked east toward the mountain.

"It looks like a hike just to get to the foothills," I said.

"It's only about three kilometers. You'll make it."

In about twenty minutes, we reached the foothills. Jorge started to veer off. "You keep going," he said. "I'm going to let these guys out."

"Why don't you leave them somewhere that we don't have to pass on the way back?" I asked.

"Do you want to carry them?" he asked.

"Fair enough," I laughed.

"Don't worry, you'll get to see more up ahead," he joked, exposing the gap between his lateral incisors.

"Why does he have a gun?" Bode asked, referring to the pistol fastened to Jorge's belt.

"No idea," I said. "Ask him."

When Jorge rejoined us Bode asked him about the gun.

"Mountain lions."

Bode and I exchanged glances and I said, "He's kidding."

"No, I'm not."

"You're taking me and my son on a walk among mountain lions?"

"That's why I have a gun," he said matter-of-factly. Several minutes passed before Jorge spoke again. "They can jump twelve meters from a standstill."

"Twelve meters? That's like forty feet. Impossible."

"And they can run seventy kilometers an hour."

"Are you trying to scare the shit out of us, Jorge?"

"Dad."

"How am I doing?" he laughed.

We continued onward for another thirty minutes before hanging a right. Jorge took the lead and Bode followed with me picking up the rear. Occasionally, a squirrel or bird or lizard would scurry across our path. Jorge would call out the name of the creature, seemingly without even looking up.

"You know where you're going?" I asked.

"Not really," he answered, "but it's hard to get lost with the ocean right there."

Since when has Jorge become a comedian, I thought to myself. Bode turned back to me and smiled. We followed Jorge's lead another kilometer or so before he made another right to head down again. After a few steps, he stopped and had us take a look at something.

"What?" I asked, not seeing anything at first.

"*Alacrán*. Scorpion," he said. "You have to be careful of the babies, like this one. They're more dangerous than the full grown ones."

"That's not full grown?"

Jorge turned to me and smiled.

"Why are the babies more dangerous?" Bode asked.

"Because when they sting, they often release more venom than the adults. Same with the *crótalos*. They're also more likely to sting in self-defense."

"Lovely," I said. "And . . . we're walking," I said in my best impersonation of a museum tour guide.

We made it back to Jorge's house without incident. I had no doubt that Jorge was serious when he said the pistol was to protect us from mountain lions, and I was pleased to not have encountered one. Bella greeted us at the house by banging her tail against the ground.

"Don't get up," I told her and scratched her behind her ear. "Bode, you hungry?"

He nodded.

"How about you, Jorge? Want to take a drive into town for lunch?"

I lifted Bella into the back of the truck, and we piled into the front. Driving into Eréndira was always more enjoyable with Jorge because he knew the locals. In his company, I felt a greater sense of warmth and acceptance, as if I wasn't just an interloper wandering around their small town.

We stopped for a bite at both my favorite places in town so we would feel more comfortable if we returned later in the week without Jorge. After a five-year absence, I had forgotten how delicious authentic Mexican food was. At the place that was someone's house-cum-restaurant, Jorge and I ordered a few *carne asada* burritos (they were much smaller than the burritos back home) and Bode dug into a bean and cheese burrito. Afterward, we stopped by the other restaurant and shared an order of guacamole with homemade tortilla chips. Gluttonous as I was when surrounded by traditional Mexican food, I ordered *carnitas* as well.

We stopped at a small market on the way back to camp. Already well stocked with water and beer, we picked up some potatoes, corn, beans, cheese, chips, and two more bags of ice. Jorge dropped us off at our campsite and I suggested he join us at sundown. As he drove away, Bella poked her head out the window and watched us grow smaller. You just knew she wanted to say something like, "Smell you later."

"How'd you like that burrito?" I asked Bode.

"Delicious."

"And the guacamole?"

"Amazing. But Dad?"

"Yeah, buddy?"

"Where's the bathroom?"

I smiled. I'd been waiting all day for that question.

"What?" his voice pitching higher.

"You've got two choices. There . . ." I nodded to a wooden outhouse that sat atop the bluff at Goats Point a few hundred meters away. ". . . or there." I nodded in the opposite direction at nothing in particular.

"*Out in the open?*"

I smiled.

"Dad."

"Come on, do you want some help?" I asked as I drained the cooler.

He nodded bashfully.

I placed the bag with the groceries onto one of tables and reached into one of the bins for the fire starter and a roll of toilet paper. I grabbed the shovel that was standing at attention at the corner of the E-Z Up and took Bode for a walk over the dunes.

"What's the shovel for?"

"You'll see."

nine

"THE STRIPES OF A TIGER are visible, but it is not so with people," Jorge said to Bode last night. "Still, you can infer what people are like by how they appear to you."

Perhaps the only reason I remember that is because it's all I scribbled into my journal before falling asleep. I was nodding off beside the campfire while Jorge was reading Bode a story from his book. All the driving and hiking had taken its toll on me, and I was wiped out. I asked Jorge to make sure Bode relieved himself before going to bed and I crawled into the tent with my journal.

Jorge had read a tale called "The Dirty Old Goblet." The moral was that it's always best to be truthful; telling lies only hurts others and ourselves, but when we tell the truth it makes the world a happier and richer place. One of the main characters in the story feigned righteousness and kindness but was actually a greedy liar. He tried to deceive a little girl by buying her golden goblet for pennies, but in the end he got exactly what he deserved. Jorge shared his own axiom about the stripes of a tiger during their post-story discussion, though I suspected he was quoting someone else. The last thing I remembered before passing out with my journal on my chest was Bode asking Jorge if he believed things were going to get worse in Tibet.

I slept unusually well and awoke in the morning fully rested. I turned to my right but Bode wasn't there again. I assumed he was already meditating, but I was still not comfortable with him leaving the tent without telling me. I crawled out to find my chair just outside the door with a note on it: *Haircut time for Bode at the house. - Jorge*

I filled the coffee pot and set it on the propane stove before taking a walk over the dunes, shovel in hand. There were two new tents set up so I walked a bit farther. When I returned, I brushed my teeth and got dressed before filling two travel mugs of coffee. I dropped a boxed apple juice into my cargo shorts and hoofed it over to Jorge's.

"Holy smokes," I said when I walked through the doorway and saw Jorge measuring Bode against the wall. "What'd you do?"

Bella followed me into the house, wagging her hindquarters. Bode was beaming as he rubbed the top of his head with both hands. "You like it?"

"Yeah, do you?"

He nodded enthusiastically and I looked at Jorge. "What'd you buzz it with?" I asked as I bent down to put the mugs on the ground and give Bella a hug.

"Bode told me last night he wanted a crew cut, so this morning I went into town and borrowed these clippers. You like it?"

"I do," I said, standing to rub his buzzed head. "Very handsome. You look twelve, though. Slow down, will you? So, how tall is he?" I asked Jorge who was penciling in a line on the wall where he marked Bode's height.

"I'm not sure, let's find something to put against the wall."

I handed him a coffee and gave the juice box to Bode. We walked around the empty house looking for something we knew the exact length of. Outside, I saw an unlabeled brown beer bottle next to one of the La-Z-Boys. Jorge, I'd noticed the previous two nights, had a habit of peeling the labels off his beers.

"Jorge, do you have the empties?"

"*Que?*"

"The empty Pacifico bottles," I said.

"*Sí*, over here," he said and walked around the side of the house to where he kept two huge heavy-duty plastic garbage cans full of empty cans and bottles.

"Jesus, Jorge. How much do you drink?"

"They're not mine. I collect them from the beach after your American friends leave them behind." He smiled wryly at me.

"Grab a few Pacificos," I suggested, quickly trying to do the math in my head. "We need like five or six of them."

Jorge looked confused but passed me three empty bottles and followed me into the house with three more. I set one on the floor beneath the mark on the wall and handed another to Bode to start stacking.

"What are you doing?" Jorge asked.

"Pacifico bottles are nine and a half inches tall."

"Should I ask how or why you know that?"

"Probably not," I said.

The bottles started to wobble on the fourth one so I helped Bode by holding the third and fourth in place while he placed a fifth one that barely touched the line that Jorge drew earlier.

"Perfect," I said. "Okay, what's five times nine and a half? Forty-five, forty-seven, forty-seven and a half," I worked out. "You're just under four feet, buddy. You're a monster!"

Bode smiled and stood at attention next to the bottles.

"That hair, dude. It's so short. Forget Budai's belly, I'm going to rub your head for good luck."

The three of us walked outside. The sun was high above the

mountains behind the house and it was beginning to warm up. I invited Jorge to breakfast, but he declined and said he would see us later. Bode and I walked back to the tent to find another two cars unloading their gear and setting up camp. I asked him if he wanted to try surfing after breakfast and he nodded.

We each had yogurt and a cereal bar beside the fire pit. While he finished his yogurt, I untied the surfboard from the truck and rubbed on some wax. I opened the tailgate and pulled out my board shorts.

"Dad!"

"What? No one can see me over the dunes," I said as I changed. Just then, a whistle came from between the dunes where yet two more cars were parked. A guy flashed me a hang loose sign and smiled behind dark glasses. I laughed and gave him a nod. "Oops," I said. "When you're done, go put your suit on and we'll head out. The waves look a bit mushy, but they'll be good to learn on."

Bode grabbed his suit from the duffle bag and went into the tent to change. So modest, I thought. "Hey buddy," I called. "Do me a favor, if you're going to leave the tent in the mornings, just wake me and tell me, okay?"

"Okay," he said and came out wearing his swimsuit and T-shirt.

"We need to get you a new bathing suit," I said.

"Why?" he asked. "It still fits."

"Yeah, but I'm not quite sure about SpongeBob," I joked.

"He probably floats," Bode said with a smile, and I spit up my last sip of coffee.

We walked over one of the dunes toward the path that led down to the shore and said hello to a guy who had just crawled out of one of the tents that had appeared overnight. Looking exhausted, the guy nodded hello before we jogged down the steep hill to the beach. The tide was out, so we walked a good twenty meters to the water's edge.

"Warm," I said as I dropped the board into the water. I had brought the only one I owned these days, a short board, but it was like a long board for Bode, which was perfect for learning.

Bode looked at me like I was crazy.

"What? It's warm. C'mon, hop on and I'll push you out."

Bode tiptoed beside the board with knocked knees and arms crossed.

"It's going to feel colder doing it that way, buddy. Just jump in and get wet and you'll feel much better." I dove into the shallow water to show him and watched as he tried to imitate me but immediately stood up shivering. "C'mon, monkey!"

Bode lay on his belly and I walked him out until the board was beside my waist.

"We can't stop the waves, but we can learn to surf," he mumbled through chattering teeth.

"What'd you just say?"

"We can't stop the waves, but we can learn to surf."

"Where'd you get that?"

"School."

"Really? Do you know what that means?"

"That when you face challenges, you can either fight them or you can embrace them."

"They taught you that in kindergarten?" I made a mental note to donate some time or money to the PTA when we got home. "That's incredible, buddy. It took me nearly thirty years to learn that lesson."

Bode shrugged and clenched the sides of the board, reminding me of myself on Eliza's boat. His shoulder blades were nearly touching and I told him to relax.

"Okay, buddy, the waves are breaking way out there, so you're going to surf the white water in, okay?"

He nodded a few times as if he was really cold, but I sensed it was nerves.

"Listen to me. First of all, we're not deep enough for you to drown. If you fall off the board, all you need to do is wait for the wave to calm down and then stand up. You're taller than the water here. Your first run, I'm simply going to push you toward the shore, and I want you to stay on your belly. Just ride the wave in, okay?"

He nodded again.

"Okay, you ready? Here we go. Remember, if you fall off, just stand up. Here you go!" I waited for the white water and pushed him along with the wave, just like when I taught him to ride his bike in the spring. He caught the wave and rode it all the way to shore. Before I could reach him, he stood up beside the board and faced me with the biggest grin on his face. At that moment, I was certain he had caught the surfing bug. We did a few more test runs with Bode boogie-boarding to shore. After about five minutes, he had lost all fear and asked if he could try to stand up.

"Okay, this time, right after my initial push, you're going to kick your feet forward and pop up. Do you want to watch me first or do you want to try?"

"I want to."

"Okay, next wave is coming, get ready."

As the whitewater drew close, I took a few steps toward shore and pushed him forward. He kicked his feet up but when he tried to stand, he immediately fell off to the right. I swam after him, but he was already standing and spitting water out of his mouth by the time I reached him.

"You all right?"

He coughed up some water but smiled broadly. "Again," he said.

We spent another hour riding the waves, during which he got up several times. Each time he got up, his determination was replenished and he wanted to go again and again. Ordinarily, I would have been happy to stay longer, but even I started to shiver, just standing in the water.

"One more, okay? I'm freezing now," I said through chattering teeth.

"Okay."

I don't know if it was the hour-long practice or pure determination, but Bode caught the last wave of the day perfectly, standing up and riding it all the way to shore. He jumped off the board just before the fins hit the sand for a perfect dismount. He turned around with his arms raised high, jumping up and down.

"That was awesome, buddy, you rock! How'd it feel?"

"Awesome!" he shouted, dancing around the board. "Did you see how long I was up?"

"I did," I said, yanking the leash from his ankle and lifting the board before the undertow took it out to sea.

We followed the path up the bluff and back to the tent. The two couples in the tents were awake and cooking a late breakfast. They congratulated Bode on his session that they'd watched from above. Bode was all smiles and skipped back to our tent.

I prepared some lunch, and we ate beside the fire pit. Afterward, Bode asked for the phone, so I grabbed it from the charger in the truck along with my journal. Bode went into the tent to avoid the glare, and I got comfortable in my chair with my feet up. I must have fallen asleep because the sound of Jorge closing the door of his truck startled me an hour or so later. I invited him to grab a couple beers out of the cooler and he took a seat beside me as Bella jumped out of the back of the truck. Bode, perhaps awake after a nap as well, crawled out of the tent and said he was going to put his feet in the water.

Once alone, Jorge asked me how Bode and I were getting on without Eliza, and I told him it was all either of us knew. He nodded and reminded me what a wonderful woman she was. I agreed, and we clinked Pacificos to Eliza. Sensing my thoughts, Jorge said, "I know it's hard to imagine, Matthew, but Eliza knew what she was doing when she chose Bode over herself. Women know things."

"I know," I said. "And I couldn't be more grateful for what she's given me, but I just wish she was here to share it." I took a sip of beer. "You know what Bode said to me earlier? We were paddling into the surf and completely out of the blue he said, 'We can't stop the waves, but we can learn to surf.' Who says that? It's things like that that I wish Eliza could hear."

"Jon Kabat-Zinn."

"What?" I said.

"Jon Kabat-Zinn said that. He's written many books about mindfulness."

"Well, he'd be pleased to know that he's got a five-year-old quoting him. The crazy thing is, he actually knew what it meant."

"He's a very special child, Matthew. I know you think he's special because he's yours, but there is something remarkable about your boy."

"He is pretty awesome."

Jorge gestured toward the ocean and I followed his gaze. "What's he doing?" he asked.

"I have no idea."

Bella also took notice and walked to the edge of the bluff and sniffed in Bode's direction.

Bode had walked out onto the rocky pier and was bending down to inspect something on the rocks. After a moment, he extended his arms and held his hands a few inches above the rocks. Though he no longer had a floppy head of hair to blow about, I could tell the wind was gusting by the ripples on the water. He closed his eyes and remained motionless for several minutes. His balance was impressive, not to mention the leg strength required to kneel for so long.

"Remarkable," Jorge said. "He's performing Reiki."

"What?"

"Reiki healing. He's sensing the energy of whatever's down there."

We watched in silence for several minutes before Jorge said, "Matthew, you're very close to your boy, but have you spent much time with other children?"

"I can't say that I have. I've been working a lot and Naja has been taking care of so much. Occasionally, I'll go to the birthday party of one of his friends, but not too often."

"Your boy is very special, Matthew."

I scoffed at his remark and finished my beer.

When Bode returned, Bella greeted him with kisses and we asked him what he'd been doing on the rocks. As Jorge surmised, he said he was feeling the energy of the clams.

"*Mejillones*?" Jorge asked.

"Mussels?" I translated.

"Black things?" Bode asked.

"Mussels," we confirmed.

"There were thousands of them," Bode remarked.

"Yes, that's where they live," I said. "I was just wondering if we should have some for dinner."

Bode frowned and then shot me a smile when Jorge said we can't.

"Why not?" I asked. "They were delicious last time."

"They're toxic in the summer."

I took his word for it.

"Do you like crab?" he asked and Bode shrugged.

"He'll eat seafood but prefers bigger fish," I said.

"Bigger fish?"

"Tell him," I said to Bode.

"Because fewer would have to die to feed us."

Bode shared his feelings about eating seafood back in the spring while walking in Winslow Park, one of Sophie's favorite jaunts. Though it had been nearly a year since Sophie had died, Bode and I would still walk the loop in the park on weekends among other dogs as a form of therapy. We dedicated those walks to learning and philosophizing about life. I encouraged Bode to use the time to talk about anything. It wasn't as if he couldn't talk to me throughout the week, it was just that our time in Winslow Park was our special time together. I started reading about Buddhism after Eliza had died and on the rare occasion he had nothing to ask, I would take the opportunity to share what I had recently learned. After all, he was learning valuable lessons nearly thirty years earlier than I had.

In a letter he sent shortly after Eliza's funeral, Jorge suggested a book called *When Things Fall Apart* by Pema Chödrön. Months earlier he had found a copy that some surfer left behind, and he suggested I read it. While the title suggests it would be a timely read for someone who had recently experienced a catastrophic event, it was much more than that. The book had an immediate and transformational effect on my entire worldview, offering insight and guidance to obtain a greater awareness and even appreciation for the hurdles we face in life. It taught me how to process everything that had happened in my life thus far and helped make sense of it all. It didn't give me my soul mate back or make the grieving process any easier, but it helped put my loss into perspective. The world as I knew it was forever changed when Eliza died, but at the same time I was given the most precious gift of all in my son. Losing my shit was not an option. With my parents gone for nearly fifteen years and no siblings to lean on, I needed to find my way and fast. Fortunately, I found it in the teachings of Buddha and his followers like Pema Chödrön.

Some people consider Buddhism their religion, but many others including myself, consider it a philosophy. One of the things I appreciate most about Buddhism is that it's all about the middle road. It's not about making sacrifices or praying to a higher power or going without like the Buddhist monks we read about. It's about finding balance in life and living in harmony with the rest of the world. A central belief in Buddhism is that all sentient beings, human or otherwise, simply want to be happy. If I live and act in accordance with what will make others happy— and they do the same—the world will be a much happier place.

Aldous Huxley once said, "I wanted to change the world. But I have found that the only thing one can be sure of changing is oneself." I believe that the teachings of Buddha have helped me gain a clearer perspective on life and have helped me change, which in some small way might just change the world. Sharing these lessons with my son, I felt, was a step in that direction.

Walking alongside a golden retriever that had befriended us while her owner walked ten or so paces behind, Bode revealed his feelings about seafood.

"Dad, I don't want shrimp scampi tonight," he said.

"I thought it's your favorite," I said.

"It is, but I don't think I want it tonight."

"Okay. Any reason why?"

Bode kicked a tennis ball that was lying on the path and the golden took off after it. "I don't know."

"What do you mean, you don't know?"

"It's just that there are so many of them. Thirty or forty, right?"

I immediately knew where he was going with this. *I shouldn't have let him help clean them last time*, I thought to myself. "Yeah?"

"That's thirty or forty shrimp that have to die for our dinner," he said.

"That's true. And very compassionate of you." I bent down so we were eye to eye. I put my hands on his shoulders. "The thought has crossed my mind as well."

"Can we have something else?"

"Of course," I said and kissed his forehead. "We had pizza last night, so I'd like to eat something healthy tonight."

"Okay. How about spinach lasagna?" he asked, evidence that my *try it seven times and you'll like it* trick had been working.

I said okay and took his hand in mine as we continued along the path. "How long do you think you'll let me hold your hand?"

"I don't know. Until I'm eighteen?"

"Eighteen? That would be great. But you'll probably be embarrassed to hold my hand sooner." I swung his hand forward and back. "But eighteen sounds good to me."

ten

I HADN'T PACKED A FISHING ROD, and evidently Jorge didn't have one. I asked him how he could possibly live in Baja without owning a rod, and he responded by saying rods were a luxury in these parts. He did, however, have the necessary supplies for creating a simple fishing rig.

Jorge had me collect a few mussels to use as bait while he went to his truck to build his contraption. While I stumbled over the rocky pier that Bode had so effortlessly navigated earlier, Bode stayed by the tent with Bella, wanting no part in our plot to kill one marine animal in order to capture another.

I returned with a handful of mussels and placed them on the open tailgate of Jorge's truck. Jorge had already secured a fishing line to an empty Pacifico bottle and was in the process of tying on a couple three-way swivels about two and four inches from the bottom of the line, where he'd already tied a lead weight. I watched as he tied two shorter pieces of line from the three-way swivels and attached hooks to each.

"We're going to catch a fish with this?" I asked, holding up the bottle in one hand and a mussel in the other. I made a mental note to bring Jorge a fishing rod on my next visit.

"If we want to eat, we will."

Jorge took out his pocketknife and wedged it between the shells of the first mussel. He worked the knife around and cut through the hinge muscle before tossing the mollusk into a small white bucket he kept in the back of the truck. After cutting open all five, he handed me the bucket and we walked down to the shore. Naturally, Bode stayed behind with Bella.

"What type of fish are we after?" I asked.

"It depends how hungry you are."

"Funny. Shall I rephrase? What kind of fish might we catch with a mussel hanging from a beer bottle?"

"Sand Perch, Ocean Whitefish, Shortfin Corvine," he said. "I suppose we might find ourselves a Roosterfish but I'm not sure we'd be able to pull one in with this, nor would we want to."

"No good?"

"*Blech.*"

Jorge had me fill the bucket with a bit of seawater to keep the mussels wet. I handed him two and placed the bucket on dry sand before we walked several paces into the surf and Jorge demonstrated how to cast the line. I turned back and looked up the bluff to see if Bode was in sight and sure enough, he was sitting cross-legged atop the hill. I waved to him, but when he didn't wave back I figured his eyes were closed and he was meditating. It was just before sunset and a prime time to fish, but Jorge was having no luck. He handed the rig to me and took a seat on the sand while I gave it a shot. We called it quits after two hours and walked the steep path up the bluff with our tails hanging between our legs. I made a joke about the effectiveness of Jorge's contraption and he just smiled.

Bode was sprawled in the sand using Bella as a pillow when we returned. I asked him what he was doing as I knelt beside the fire pit to build a fire.

"Watching a movie."

"What movie," I asked. "*E.T.*?"

"*SpongeBob*," he said without looking up.

"Super," I replied at the absurdity of it. One minute he's meditating, and the next he's watching *SpongeBob SquarePants*.

"What's for dinner?"

"Not fish."

That caught his attention. He appeared confused as to what we were going to eat, but then cracked a smile at my misfortune. "*Cheesadilla*?"

"*Cheesadillas* all around," I said. "We'll cook up some beans, too."

The last light of the day was gone by the time we threw our paper plates into the fire. Jorge didn't stay for dinner, but he returned shortly after with another bundle of firewood. He grabbed a beer from the cooler and then pulled Bode's empty chair closer to the fire. Bode was reclined on my lap and following along as I read to him.

"I was just reading the introduction to Bode," I said, holding up the storybook.

"What have you learned so far, *muchacho*?"

"Not much. It seems very simple."

Jorge nearly fell out of his chair laughing. "Really?" he asked.

"It's one of the first things we learned in kindergarten," he said. "Treat everything the way you want to be treated. If everyone did, everyone would be happier, right?"

"Very true," Jorge said.

"And what about The Four Noble Truths?" I asked. "What do you think about those?"

"They make sense," he said and paused for a moment. "Remember that time I cried because you wouldn't buy me a new Matchbox car?"

"You didn't just cry, Bode. You had a complete meltdown."

"Was I acting like a baby?"

"Yes," I laughed.

"It's like that," he said. "Even though I had a million cars at home, I wanted another one. And when I didn't get one, I got upset."

"So, what do you think that means?" I asked, smiling at Jorge to watch this.

"It means that I should be grateful for what I have because a lot of kids don't have any cars."

"What else?"

He thought for a moment. "That if I continue to want more and more cars, I'll be disappointed when I don't get them."

I kissed him on the top of his head. "You're a good boy. And I've got news for you: there are many adults who don't understand that simple lesson. When they don't get the car they want, they also get upset."

"It doesn't mean that I can't have cars, right?"

"Right. It just means that if you're greedy or become attached to the cars, you're only setting yourself up for disappointment. Or suffering, as Buddha called it."

"I can still love the cars I have, though."

"Of course. Just be grateful for having them. And know that they are temporary."

"What do you mean?"

I considered whether *impermanence* was a lesson he would grasp.

Jorge interjected. "One day a friend will want to borrow one of your cars or you'll lose one or it will simply break. That is the nature of things."

"Nothing lasts forever," I said. "And while it's perfectly natural to feel sad when you lose something, it's something entirely different to not expect it."

"Like Sophie."

I kissed his head again. "Yes, like Sophie."

"And Mom."

I rested my lips on his head. "And Mom."

Jorge removed two beers from the cooler and popped the caps with a lighter he kept in his shirt pocket. He handed me one as he took his seat. Bode remained silent, presumably taking in the lesson that I thought might have been too much for one night.

"Dad?"

"Yeah, buddy?"

"Do you miss Mom?"

"More than anything."

After several minutes of gazing at the stars and listening to crackling of the fire, Jorge spoke. "*Muchacho*, I brought something to show you." He removed a small object from his shirt pocket. At first I thought it was his lighter, but it was something else. He held it with two fingers and it flickered in the firelight. "It's called a *vajra*." He handed it to Bode and said, "It's a ritual item that represents the compassion of all the Buddhas."

Bode held the *vajra* with two hands and twirled it in the firelight. It was made of metal, likely bronze, and three or four inches in length. The center was a small sphere and from opposite sides emerged two eight-petal flowers, which—we've since looked up—represent lotuses.

"A friend picked it up in Nepal and gave it to me many years ago. I didn't know what it symbolized back then but I've since learned that *vajra* means *thunderbolt*. Some say it represents the thunderbolt experience of Buddhist awakening or enlightenment, which, now that I think about it, is called *bodhi*."

"Like my name."

"Yes, but spelled differently," I said.

"The *vajra* is known to destroy ignorance, yet is indestructible, itself. I would like you to have it."

"Jorge—"

He held his hand up and shook his head.

"Really?" Bode looked at me and I smiled. "Thank you, *Señor Espinoza*," he said, drawing a chuckle out of Jorge. He crawled off my lap and gave Jorge a hug. "Thank you," he repeated.

Jorge smiled at me over Bode's shoulder.

"What do you say you brush your teeth and put on your PJs? It's getting late."

While Bode was getting ready for bed, I thanked Jorge for his gift.

"That is one special boy, Matthew. I've never seen anything like it."

"Jorge, you live in Punta Cabras. How many kids do you see around here?"

"You forget that I raised a son myself. And I didn't always live here, you know. That boy is remarkable."

Bode returned in his gray bedtime sweatpants and white T-shirt. He had outgrown the sweatpants and they only reached the top of his ankles but they were his favorite. His headlamp was lit and his toothbrush stuck out of his mouth.

"Don't forget to pee, buddy," I said shielding the light from his headlamp.

He nodded and walked into the darkness.

"Not near someone else's tent," I joked and took a sip of beer.

When Bode returned, he asked if I would tuck him in. He said good night to Jorge and I followed him into the tent.

"Did you have fun surfing today?"

He nodded.

"Wanna catch a fish with me tomorrow?"

He shook his head.

"Fair enough. Sleep well, handsome. Don't grow too much tonight."

"Okay."

I kissed him on the forehead. "I love you. Sweet dreams."

"Sweet dreams."

"He's lucky to have a father like you," Jorge said when I returned to the campfire.

"It's just part of my job."

"You do a good job."

Jorge and I stayed up late and drank too many beers. He couldn't get over Bode's ability to grasp lessons that many adults failed to master in a lifetime. He kept describing him as "remarkable" and "special" which I continued to dismiss, though I was secretly proud. Truth is, I did feel that Bode was well beyond his years spiritually, but I attributed it to my parenting style and my commitment to sharing the teachings I was just discovering for myself. Some parents place a basketball in their baby's crib, others insist on piano lessons until their child's fingers bleed. I simply gave Bode a head start of another kind. I figured that if he could learn to use his inside voice while indoors and to never run with scissors, why not teach him other life lessons? I saw no reason to wait for him to experience heartbreak or tragedy in order to understand they are inherently part of our existence. I'd be lying if I said I wasn't surprised that Bode learned these lessons as swiftly as he did, but I wasn't complaining. Labeling him gifted, however, was a bit much for me, so I steered our conversation toward Jorge's family.

Not much had changed with Ana and Pablo, Jorge told me. Ana was working for the same family in Encino and was getting along well. She worked hard, managing a house with three children and a farm's worth of pets, but she sounded content in all her letters, he said. Most Saturdays, she would take the bus to meet Pablo for lunch. Pablo had recently earned his culinary arts degree in Los Angeles and was working as a sous chef at a French restaurant in Century City. Jorge lamented that Pablo didn't write often, so he was enthusiastic about the prospect of communicating more frequently via the tablet.

I must have fallen asleep beside the fire because Jorge woke me with a squeeze of the shoulder before heading back to his house. I crawled into the tent quietly so I wouldn't disturb Bode. I kissed his temple and slipped into my sleeping bag. As I got comfortable, I recalled Jorge's gap-toothed smile and how happy he appeared at the thought of seeing his family again. My thoughts quickly turned to Eliza and as I spooned Bode, I wondered if I would ever love another woman so deeply again.

eleven

BODE UNZIPPED THE tent around ten to provide my second wake-up call of the morning. I had every intention of getting up and starting the coffee when he woke me earlier, but as soon as he zipped the door shut behind him, I was out once again.

"We need to scatter Sophie's ashes," he said, crawling into the tent. "Dad?"

I waited for him to come closer.

"Dad?" He crawled closer. "Dad, you up?" He placed a hand on my shoulder.

With a roar, I grabbed him and tackled him to the ground. I kissed his neck and tickled him all over until he cried uncle. We lay in the tent while Bode caught his breath, and I assessed the extent of my hangover.

"Are we going to scatter Sophie's ashes?" he said.

"We probably should. After breakfast?"

"Okay."

There was a bit of a chill in the air, and the skies were cloudy and gray. I put the coffee on the stove and grabbed a juice box and yogurt from the cooler while brushing my teeth.

"Did you brush?" I mumbled.

He nodded.

"Good boy," I said, toothpaste spittle flying everywhere. "*Ruff*!" I did my best imitation of a rabid dog and chased him out of his seat.

"You're silly, Dad."

I grabbed the shovel and told Bode I'd be back in a minute. He sat back down on his chair and began flipping through his storybook. When I returned, I noticed what he was wearing—a hooded sweatshirt, bathing suit, and Ugg boots. He had only been surfing for a day but already looked the part. He sat on the chair facing the ocean as if contemplating a morning session despite the chill and mushy waves. It was a common scene along the California coast throughout the year—surfers wearing hoodies, gazing out at the ocean, and weighing their options, the pros and cons of a quick session before work. I gave his shoulder a squeeze as I walked to the truck to grab some clothing. I dressed beside the tent, filled my mug with coffee, and joined Bode.

"Should we build a fire?" I asked.

"Maybe after Sophie."

I smiled. "Has Jorge been by this morning?"

He shook his head.

We ate a small breakfast quietly under the weight of the impending ceremony. I gazed out at the Pacific and reflected on Sophie's life. I was just twenty-two when I adopted her from a breeder somewhere in Pennsylvania. I remember my small one bedroom in Manhattan and how my friends said that a New York City apartment was too small for a dog, especially a big dog like a golden retriever. I contended that dogs don't run in apartments, that she'd get her exercise in the park before and after work and that she'd sleep most of the day. I thought about the various dog walkers I had hired over the years and the doggie day care we sent her to after Eliza moved in and we could afford the additional expense.

"Are you thinking about Sophie?"

"Quit it, dude."

Bode giggled. "What are you laughing at?"

"That your mom and I spent $400 a month on doggie day care. It was only a little more expensive than a dog walker but $400 *a month*. She was worth it, though."

"Did she like it?"

"I hope so. It made me feel better that she was looked after and playing all day. But now, I'm not sure whether she enjoyed it. Dogs like to sleep a lot, and I'm not sure she had much chance at daycare. I wonder if she viewed it as playing, or just being stuck in a brownstone with a bunch of other dogs."

"I'm sure she was happy."

Bode and I walked hand in hand over the dunes and down the path to the beach. I recalled Sophie's last few weeks. We had gone camping in upstate New York one weekend, and the drive up was over ninety-five degrees. We stopped for a quick rest at a supermarket in a small town before the campground. I opened the back of the truck to let Sophie out but she just stood there, peering down at the ground. I lifted her up and placed her on the ground but she just stood motionless for a moment and then began to walk very slowly and deliberately, as if she were blind. She seemed dizzy and couldn't walk a straight line. I was concerned that she might have suffered a heat stroke so I walked her to a shady patch of grass next to the asphalt. After she relieved herself, her gait seemed to improve but she was still wobbly. Bode placed her bowl in the shade and I filled it with water. I encouraged her to drink but she only took a sip. There was no need to tie her up, but I attached her leash to her collar and dropped it deliberately next to her—a command to stay that we've agreed on over the years. Bode and I quickly ran into the market to pick up a few items. When we returned, I was pleased to see Sophie drinking from her bowl. We sat beside her for a few minutes and when I said, "Ready?" she popped right up.

I drove the remaining way to the campground with the A/C blasted. When we arrived at the campsite, Sophie jumped out of the truck and explored the site and its smells as usual before taking a seat in the shade. I filled her water bowl and placed it in the shade of the picnic table and watched as she strolled over to take a drink. Her gait seemed better but she remained uncharacteristically lethargic the entire weekend.

I remember Bode and Sophie resting in the tent after a long, uphill walk back from the park's lake. We had the fly off the tent because it was so hot, and I could see Bode and Sophie resting on top of the sleeping bags. I didn't think much about it at the time, but I remember Sophie sprawled out on her side next to Bode, who had one hand above her head, as if he was about to feel her forehead for temperature. Instead of touching her, he just held his hand an inch or so away from her. I observed this for about two minutes before some fellow campers—a couple and their daughter—stopped at our site to say hello. They saw us walk by earlier and wondered if they could pet Sophie. The young girl seemed to be a couple years older than Bode and was several inches taller. Bode showed her how Sophie liked to hold hands and that got the girl giggling and her mother cooing.

"I guess we're getting a golden," the father joked to no one in particular.

When the family continued on their walk, Bode asked me to take a look at Sophie's face, which seemed to droop a bit on one side. I took a picture of her but didn't have a signal on the phone so I couldn't send it, not that the vet would have received it until after the weekend.

During our visit the following Monday, the vet suggested it was a brain tumor. He said that without conducting expensive tests, he couldn't be certain of his diagnosis, but he was sufficiently convinced. As he turned to scribble in Sophie's chart, I heard him say under his breath that he hoped it would be fast.

He offered to conduct the tests but recommended otherwise. Gesturing to the framed paintings of black Labs on the walls—no less than six of them—he explained that he'd owned retrievers his entire life and this was how they died. Sophie had lived a full life, though shorter than I had been prepared for, and it would be a matter of weeks. I declined the tests. We agreed the best course of action was to keep her comfortable for as long as possible. I asked how I would know when it was time and he asked if I had had Sophie since she was a puppy. When I nodded yes, he simply said, "You'll know."

By the shimmer of the sand on the shore, I determined the tide was on its way out which was good. The thought of scattering Sophie's remains from a precarious position on the rocks only for them to wash ashore was disheartening. Holding the plastic canister containing Sophie's ashes in one hand, I only had the other to break a possible fall. I placed a hand on Bode's shoulder and encouraged him to lead. We made our way to the tip of the pier and took a seat on the last two flat boulders.

"So," I said, removing the plastic bag from the canister.

"So," Bode repeated.

Immediately, a wave of sadness washed over me. Bode put his arm around me and leaned his head against my shoulder. I lifted my arm and brought him closer.

"She was a good dog, wasn't she, buddy?"

"Yep."

Clearly, I was going to do most of the talking.

"Sophie was a good dog," I said again and cleared my throat, unsure how to give a eulogy for a dog. "She made so many people happy, especially your mom." I squeezed Bode's elbow. "Did you know your mom was afraid of thunderstorms?"

"That's silly."

"I know, but she hated them. I think it was the only thing in the world your mom was afraid of. Sophie didn't like them either. The two of them would cuddle in bed together anytime there was a thunderstorm. They were pretty cute."

"Mom loved Sophie as much as me?"

"You have no idea. Sophie gave your mom so much attention that it would have been impossible not to fall in love with her. And she became super protective of your mom, especially after Mom got pregnant."

Bode wiggled to get comfortable and returned his head to my shoulder.

"Your mom used to run with Sophie in the morning before work. This one time, a couple weeks before you were born, they were walking up the hill on Cross Highway on the way home from a morning walk, and Sophie started to growl at some guy who was walking toward them, though your mom didn't understand why."

"The stripes of a tiger are visible, but it is not so with people."

I looked at him and smiled. "How do you do that? How do you remember stuff like that?"

He shrugged, and I gave him a squeeze.

"Anyway, this time when your mom and Sophie were walking home, the leash went taut and your mom instinctively followed Sophie across the street. As they passed the man, he turned around and started walking back up the hill. Your mom saw him trying to pull even with her and Sophie started to bark and pull at the leash. Your mom didn't want the guy to follow them to the house so she turned around and started back the way she had come."

"Did he follow?"

"Yep. So your mom picked up the pace and walked back to Main Street and over to Coffee An'. She left Sophie outside and walked in and stood by the window. When the man came by, Sophie started to bark like crazy. He inched closer, as if he was going to pet her but your mom cracked open the door and asked him to leave Sophie alone. She said the guy gave her a creepy smile and continued walking."

"What happened to the man?"

"We're not sure. She never saw him again."

Bode sat quietly for a moment before concluding, "Sophie was a good dog." Bode smiled and tossed a shell he found into the water. "She was a good swimmer, too."

"She was. She loved the water. She even loved bath time."

"I like bath time."

"Of course you do. But she was a dog. Dogs don't usually like the bath."

We sat and stared at the water. I pulled my pocketknife from my cargo shorts and opened the blade. "What do you think?" I asked.

Bode nodded, and I pressed the tip of the knife into the plastic bag and cut a hole at the top. I looked at Bode. He was expressionless, staring at the water beneath his dangling feet. Behind him in the distance I spotted someone on the top of the bluff watching us. Jorge. He gave a nod and turned away.

"Well, Sophie," I croaked. "You were a great dog. You made us all so happy, and we miss you terribly. You loved the water more than anything so we figured we'd set you free here."

Delivering a eulogy for a person had been much easier. Eliza's funeral was by far the worst day of my life but I still managed to keep it together until after the eulogy. Out on the pier with

Bode, I could hardly utter another word.

"Goodbye, Sophie," Bode said. "Meet some new friends."

I looked at him and laughed through my tears. "Meet some new friends?"

He nodded.

I cupped my hand around his shoulder and gave it a squeeze. I stretched the hole at the top of the bag a bit wider and slowly poured the remains into the blue water. "Meet some new friends, Sophie."

We sat for several minutes and watched the ashes create a gray cloud just beneath the surface. The cloud bobbed back and forth, swaying with the ripples that softly kissed the rocks below. Tiny slivers near the water's surface sparkled in the sunlight as the murky mass remained intact, waiting obediently it seemed, for one final command.

"Bye, Sophie," Bode said. "Until we meet again."

I put my arm around him and pulled him onto my lap. Wiping my tears on the shoulder of his sweatshirt, I kissed his hooded head and hugged him tight. Ever so slowly, the cloud stretched into the ocean. We watched solemnly, staring until we were no longer certain the faint streak was still there, or just an imprint in our minds.

twelve

THE SCATTERING OF SOPHIE'S ashes weighed heavily on me for much of the day. The sun seemed to mourn as well, rarely emerging from behind thick clouds. A chill remained in the air, and the campfire that Jorge had started in our absence was a welcoming sight. The old man sat in one of the chairs with a steaming cup of coffee in hand and a faint smile. I placed a hand on his shoulder as I walked to the E-Z Up to blow my nose and grab a noon beer. Bode took a seat in the sand next to Bella who was resting comfortably beside the fire.

I felt like being by the water so I decided to give fishing another shot. I invited Bode to join me and when he declined, Jorge gave me a nod indicating that I should go while he stayed back with Bode.

I made my way to the beach and placed both beer bottles— the fishing rig included—onto the sand. I carefully walked onto the pier to pick a couple mussels. *Which ones, Sophie?* I thought. I felt her presence, and it lifted my spirits as I twisted two mussels from the rock. Perhaps she would bring me some luck. Once again, I negotiated the jagged rocks and made my way back to shore before flipping open my knife and prying one of the mussels open. I sliced it free from the shell and attached it to both hooks.

I reacquainted myself with the casting motion, and I shortly found my form. Casting a line from a beer bottle wasn't pretty, but it did the trick. The undertow was strongest beside the pier so I remained close and timed my cast as the water receded and watched as the line was carried out.

After twenty minutes standing nearly motionless, a dull pain surfaced in my lower back so I grabbed the bucket and walked back out onto the pier where Bode and I sat earlier.

I cast the line into deeper water and closed my eyes. Another half hour passed without so much as a nibble. "What do you think, Sophie, is Jorge messing with me?" Just then I felt a firm tug on the line. More out of surprise than fishing acumen, I yanked the bottle skyward and set the hook. I was so surprised to have actually hooked something that, until that moment, I hadn't even considered how to reel such a contraption. I held the bottle horizontally, as if it was a kite's spool, and rotated it to draw in the line. The tension actually helped the line grip against the bottle, but rotating it proved incredibly difficult. I knew the odds were slim but decided to try to walk the fish to shore while doing my best to reel. I made a futile attempt to call out to Jorge; my voice was nothing compared to the sound of the wind and ocean. I took one step at a time, taking care to avoid unnecessarily tugging on the line. I made my way to the shore and hopped off the last rock onto the sand. Standing on *terra firma*—or perhaps because the fish had lost some of its will—I found it a bit easier to rotate the bottle. Still, at the rate I was reeling, it would take an hour to bring the fish to hand.

I called out again to Jorge and Bode, but neither appeared at the top of the bluff. I took a step backward and then another. The fish remained on the line for ten paces, but I was out of real estate, my back against the bluff. I couldn't imagine the fish being too far off and considered for a moment how to bring it in.

Placing the bottle on the ground and securing it with my foot, I yanked off my sweatshirt. With the bottle on the sand, I gripped the line with the sleeves of my sweatshirt and gave it a couple slow and steady pulls. Just then I caught my first glimpse of the fish flailing in the shallow water. A rush of adrenaline came over me as it breached the surface and I pulled hand over hand four more times until the fish was finally on shore. I rushed over and lifted it by the line. The fish was a good 18 to 20 inches long and silver. Its mouth was large, and its lower jaw projected further than its upper. Small razor-like teeth lined the perimeter of its yellow mouth, and I kept a watchful eye as it writhed on the line. Just as I was placing it in the bucket, the fish dislodged itself from the hook and fell perfectly into the bucket, nearly folding in half. I filled the container with some water like they did on the chartered fishing boats I used to go on with my dad as a kid.

While walking toward the path that led up the bluff, I spotted Jorge peering down and smiling. I tilted the bucket to give him a look.

"What do you have there?" he asked when I made it back to the campsite.

"Dinner!"

"Ah, wonderful, a Shortfin Corvine," he said. "Delicious."

"Excellent, you're cooking tonight." I placed the bucket beside the cooler and pulled the bottle from my cargo shorts. "I can't believe this thing actually worked." I tossed it in the sand beside the fire pit and collapsed into a chair. "How you doing, handsome?"

"Fine," Bode replied, still beside Bella.

"How's Bella?"

"Okay."

"Wanna see the fish I caught?"

"Nah."

"Nah? *Nah*?" I leapt off the chair and tackled him on the sand.

"Dad!" he squealed.

"Want to take a ride into town?"

"Okay."

Jorge stayed behind with Bella while Bode and I drove into town. We stopped for a couple burritos and picked up some more ice for the cooler. When we returned, Jorge and Bella were down on the shore, and I asked Bode if he wanted to surf. We slipped into our bathing suits and joined Jorge on the beach. Bella was excited and pranced between us before we waded into the ocean. She dipped her paws but stayed on shore.

The water felt much colder with the sun hidden behind the clouds and we could taste the salt as we waded out to the whitewater. We stayed out for the better part of an hour until I started to shiver. Bode got up for a few seconds on nearly every attempt. Each time he emerged from the water, he turned and smiled triumphantly with arms overhead. Maybe he was a surfer *and* a climber, I thought. Jorge sat in the sand beside Bella and applauded after each wave.

The embers in the fire pit were still hot when we returned to the tent. The plan was to leave the next day and, thanks to Jorge, we had plenty of wood to burn. We built up the fire and relaxed with our feet on the rocks of the fire ring.

"I went to Coyote Cal's earlier and spent some time on the Internet," Jorge said.

"What's happening in the world?"

"Not sure. I was just looking up some things."

"Like what?" I asked.

"I looked up *heterochromia* whatever—"

"*Heterochromia iridum*," I said.

"It's very interesting. Did you know Alexander the Great had it?"

"No, but lots of people have it."

"Like Mila Kunis," Bode chimed in.

"Who?" Jorge asked.

"An American actress Bode has a crush on." I shot Bode a smile.

Jorge smiled, too, and Bode looked bashfully down toward Bella.

"Does he suffer from any other conditions? *Heterochromia—*"

"*Iridum.*"

"Is often a sign of something else."

"One day with Google and you're a doctor?" I laughed. "No, he's fine. He's been tested for a whole slew of things but he's perfectly fine."

"Only fine?" Bode asked.

"Better than fine. He's perfect." I grinned at Bode. "His mom had partial *heterochromia*. It wasn't too noticeable. But if you looked closely, you would see that her left eye had some brown around her hazel iris."

"It's hereditary then?"

"His is, yes."

"Interesting." Jorge sat back as if contemplating something.

I bit. "What's up?"

"Who is Bode named after?"

"His great-grandfather," I said. "Hubert was Eliza's grandfather's name. She was very close with him when she was young. We knew we would never call him Hubert, though, so we chose a middle name that we both liked. Bode was one of the few we could agree on."

"Do you know what his name means?" Jorge asked.

"*Bodhi* means *awakening*, doesn't it? *Awakening* or *enlightened*, right? But it's not spelled the same as Bode."

"Of course, but I was talking about Hubert. Look here," he said as he passed the iPad. "Hubert comes from the German elements *hugu* meaning *heart, mind, spirit*, and *berht* meaning *bright, famous*."

"That's cool. I'm pretty sure we didn't look it up when naming him, though. Eliza simply wanted to name him after her grandfather."

"Was Eliza's grandfather German?"

"Polish. He was an extraordinary man. He owned some kind of business—shoes or leather or something. During the war, he helped protect an entire family by hiding them in the basement of the store. It was a family of seven or nine. It's how he met his wife, Eliza's grandmother, Sarah. She was the oldest daughter."

"Interesting," Jorge said, watching Bode scratch Bella behind the ear. "That's not it, though."

"What's not it?"

"His name. Bode, spelled b-o-d-e, has a special meaning, too."

"Of course it does," I jested. "What else did you learn, Dr. Espinoza?"

"Bode is derived from the Old English *bodian* or *boda*."

"Let me guess, it means *remarkable one*," I joked.

"It means *messenger*."

"Messenger of what?"

"Just *messenger*." Jorge gazed out to the Pacific and we sat quietly for a moment.

I laughed and stood up, using Jorge's shoulder as leverage. "I've got to see a man about a horse."

When I returned, Jorge was cleaning the fish and Bode had

the cooler open. "Whatcha looking for?" I asked.

"The corn and potatoes," he said.

I rubbed his crew cut and showed him where they were. "We'll make some extra potatoes so we can make home fries in the morning."

"Okay," he said. "How about the corn? Naked or not naked?" He held up a cob.

"Let's go with naked," I said. "They're gonna be hot so let's remove the husks first."

Bode got to work on the corn while I stabbed the potatoes a few times with my knife and wrapped them in foil before nestling them in the coals. Let's put a little butter on the corn before we wrap them."

I poured a bit of olive oil into a pan and handed it to Jorge whom already had the fish filleted.

"Your potatoes will be in there for quite a while, no?" he said. "Once the flames come down, the fire will be fine for the fish. We'll start cooking it when you put the corn on."

I filled two paper cups with a cylinder of ice and couple fingers of scotch, and grabbed an apple juice for Bode. After handing a drink to Jorge, I motioned for Bode to stand for a second. I pulled the chair close to the fire and sat down, pulling him onto my lap.

"You okay, big guy?"

He nodded.

"You okay with eating the fish tonight?"

He nodded again.

"Will you ever eat my scampi again?" I asked.

Bode shrugged.

A few moments passed before Jorge pointed out, "You can always buy jumbo shrimp."

Bode spit out his juice with an unexpected chortle, which made Jorge and me burst out laughing.

"You're a good boy, you know that?" I squeezed him close and kissed his head.

"Crab grow pretty large, too, you know," Jorge said.

"Here it comes," I groaned.

"Your dad loves crab," he said, shooting me a toothless smile.

"And, there it is. You almost went a whole visit without making that joke. She didn't give me crabs, *culo*. My wet suit gave me a rash." I sipped my scotch and recalled the girl who joined me on my first visit to Baja.

Jorge guffawed at his own joke. It took him four days, but he'd finally found a way to work his quip into our conversation. He had been telling the same joke for nearly fifteen years and had clearly been struggling. Bode looked at me and I just shook my head.

"Don't listen to this old man," I said and then relented and gave Jorge the satisfaction of a smile. He worked hard for it.

Bode seemed to enjoy dinner but only shrugged when I asked him how the fish tasted. He ate everything on his plate, and I took comfort in the fact he wouldn't go hungry that evening. We tossed our plates in the fire, and Bode ambled over to the edge of the bluff and sat facing the water. Bella, who hadn't moved more than three feet in hours, stretched her old legs and joined him. Jorge and I exchanged glances and smiled. I reached into the cooler for a couple cylinders of ice and dropped them into each of our cups before pouring a few more fingers. Jorge gave me an "enough" gesture but it was too late.

"There's a storm coming," he said.

"How can you tell?"

"The wind. It's coming from the wrong direction. Something's brewing."

"Are you sure you didn't check weather.com?" I joked.

"Twenty-five years on this beach, my friend. I don't need a website to tell me when to go inside."

"Fair enough. Do you think it will come tonight?"

"Perhaps. My guess is tomorrow."

"Not one of those sandstorms, I hope."

Years ago—after Brett's wedding in L.A.—Eliza and I experienced our first sandstorm during a visit to Baja. I had been in the middle of an epic surf session when massive gray clouds suddenly overtook the sky. It was as if Eliza, who had been tanning contently on the shore, was watching me surf on the DVR and hit fast-forward to get to the dramatic part. The wind didn't feel unusually strong while I was in the water, but the darkening sky was warning enough. By the time I caught the next wave, the rain was coming down horizontally. We rushed up the bluff together and started throwing everything in the back of the truck. The wind intensified and began taking everything that wasn't bolted down.

Even the most enthusiastic campers will tell you that there are very few things in life that are worse than camping in the rain. Not only do things get wet that shouldn't—and never seem to dry before your trip is over—you are confined to your tent whether it's time for bed or not. And forget about getting any kind of sleep should you be unfortunate enough to have a leak in your tent.

During that visit to Punta Cabras, Eliza and I discovered one of those things that were, indeed, worse than camping in the rain: camping in a rainy *sandstorm*. A sandstorm itself wouldn't have been so bad. Sure, sand gets everywhere, including your eyes, making you want to crawl into your tent and pry your eyeballs out with your Leatherman. But that's nothing compared to the pure agony of a rainy sandstorm. Not only do you get sand in your eyes, ears, nose, and every other orifice, the granules stick to everything: tent and sleeping bags, cooler, coffee pot, pots and pans, mugs, the grooves of the flashlight switch, the trigger of the fire starter, the plastic contraption that lets you adjust the size of your headlamp band, even between the tines of forks. While the sandstorm itself might last just a few hours, you are doomed to contend with its aftereffects for many trips to come.

Our backpacks were in the tent so it hadn't yet blown away. As the storm intensified, however, it was clear that if we didn't do something our belongings would be toast, likely blown over the edge of the bluff and into the Pacific. While Eliza hurried to throw everything she could into the back of the truck, I dove into the tent to prevent it from being swept away. I heard the door slam shut, so I figured Eliza was safely inside as I lay prone in a figure X for what seemed like an eternity, praying to stay grounded.

Though I had never previously experienced a sandstorm, I figured it couldn't last more than an hour or so. I was mistaken. The rain continued to come down in sheets well into the evening, not that it could have gotten any darker. The wind pressed so heavily on the tent that the roof, typically four feet high, hovered just inches above my body. The sound of the storm was downright frightening. I remained hunkered down, spread like a snow angel, for as long as possible. Each time I flipped from my stomach to my back it felt as if the tent was going to take off. I waited out the storm as long as possible. And then the leak began.

I was more uncomfortable than I had ever been in my life, and the dripping water made it a thousand times worse. Wet, sandy, and sweaty in the steamy tent, I sat for a few minutes and devised my plan. I tossed loose clothing and gear into our backpacks and pushed them toward one zippered door while I wiggled out the other into the driving rain and sand. With my eyes squinted nearly shut, I hurried to collapse the tent. I folded the flat side of the tent over the backpacks, picked up the entire bundle and hobbled to the truck. I figured the back of the truck would be completely packed so I went around to the rear side door. It was *locked*. I cursed everything that was holy and dropped the gear in the wet sand. I unwrapped the tent, found the open zipper and burrowed my head and shoulders into it to search for the keys. After checking nearly every pocket, I realized that Eliza probably had the keys and, more importantly, had already unlocked the truck after hearing me try to get in. I crawled out of the tent, picked up the bundle once again and opened the back door. The cooler was in the backseat—*why?* I asked myself, it was the one thing that was heavy and waterproof—so I pushed it across to the other side before shoving in the gear. I threw the door closed, jumped into the front seat and slammed my door. Out of breath, I sat for a minute with my eyes closed and burning, pondering what it may have been that cracked when I shoved the cooler. I turned to the right, about to investigate what it was, and discovered a dry and toasty Eliza, grinning from ear to ear.

"You're thinking about your first sandstorm, yes?" Jorge asked.

I smiled and took a sip of scotch. "You never forget your first," he said.

With that, I put down my cup and took a quick inspection of the kitchen area. The bins were heavy and in no danger of flying off in a storm. I stole a glance at Jorge, and he smiled. With everything in order, I rejoined Jorge beside the fire.

"I just hope we're packed up before it arrives," I said. "I have no desire to find sand in everything when Bode I go camping this fall."

Jorge smiled and sipped his drink. "When are you planning on leaving?"

"Crossing the border isn't too bad just after noon, so we'll probably head out after breakfast. Unless we have to pack up earlier."

Jorge nodded.

Bode joined us at the fire, and I asked him to grab some chocolate from the cooler. I asked if either of them wanted s'mores and both said no. I held up a Hershey's bar and, again, both declined. *Who are these people?* I thought. Bode couldn't get comfortable on the cooler, so I motioned for him to sit on my lap. We sat quietly, listening to the crackling wood and staring at the ribbons of fire as they danced in the wind of the brewing storm.

thirteen

THE FLUTTERING FLY woke us early. Perhaps I should have staked it to the ground, but years ago I had made the determination that creating a vestibule with the fly is only good for two things: keeping a wet dog out of the tent yet sheltered from the elements, and providing one more thing to stub your toe on. Considering I had not the dog, nor the inclination to stub my toe, I opted for no unnecessary stakes.

I pulled Bode close and spooned him for a while as the wind gusted outside. The last morning of a camping trip is a sad one. It wasn't the breaking down of the tent or the meticulous packing of gear; it is merely the end of a good thing. Living simply, with no responsibilities other than basic survival, is a luxury. It was still two weeks away but my thoughts wandered to the position waiting for me at 4.0. I caught myself, however, let my thoughts go, and buried my face in Bode's neck.

"I don't want to get up," I said after a few minutes.

I couldn't tell if Bode had fallen back asleep.

"I . . . don't . . . want . . . to . . . get . . . up," I croaked into his neck while giving him a good squeeze.

"Dad!"

"I don't want to get up!" I roared and began tickling him all over.

"Daddy!" he squealed.

"I don't want to get up!"

"Dad, stop! I'm gonna pee!"

That made me laugh. It was a magic word even more powerful than *uncle,* and I stopped at once. I hovered over him and gave him kisses all over his head, cheeks and neck. He squirmed and complained of my scratchy beard.

"Did you grow again? I hope you didn't grow!"

"Yes!" he shouted proudly.

"No, stop growing! I like you small. Stop growing and stay little!"

I kissed him again and squirmed out of the sleeping bag. I unzipped the tent door and poked my head out. It didn't look like a storm with the turquoise sky and big puffy clouds, but the wind was howling.

"Let's get dressed and build a bonfire with the rest of the wood," I suggested.

We dressed in the tent and after setting the coffee pot on the stove and starting the fire, we walked quietly over the dunes and passed a few tents to our designated latrine area. Of course, we may have walked through other people's designated latrine areas but what could you do? We did our business and returned to a blazing fire and freshly brewed pot of coffee. We brushed our teeth and sat upwind of the fire with coffee and milk in hand.

"Can I try your coffee?"

"Sure, give me your milk. My dad used to do this for me." I poured a bit of coffee into his milk and handed it back. "I used to call this *coffee milk*. Very original, I know, but I used to have it every weekend when I was about your age. I thought I was so grown up."

He smiled. "It tastes like that ice cream you get."

"Coffee mocha chip?"

He nodded and took another sip, forming a milk mustache. I smiled and ran my hand back and forth over his crew cut.

"Jorge did a good job with this. You still like it?"

"I guess. I haven't really seen it since he buzzed it."

"That's right. Wait a sec." I retrieved the phone from the car. "Smile." I snapped the photo with the fire in the background and the Pacific beyond. I handed it to Bode.

"Nice," he said, rubbing the top of his head.

"You can see your eyes now."

He examined my face for any subtext.

"Bode, your eyes are incredible. You needn't be self-conscious. Trust me, people would give anything for your eyes."

"But two different colors?"

"Bode, it's no fun being like everyone else. Your eyes are incredible. You're very lucky."

"You said there's no such thing as luck, that you make your own."

"Well, I lied," I said with a smile. "You're going to have all the girls chasing after you."

He hung his head and smiled bashfully. Just then we heard the sound of a car door. We hadn't heard the engine over the wind and crackling fire, and we turned to see Jorge walking to the back of his truck to open the tailgate for Bella. Clearly excited, Bella did a stutter-step before jumping out the back and catching up to Jorge who approached with a great big toothless smile.

"Good morning, Dr. Espinoza. How goes it?"

"*Buenos dias, muchachos.* A glorious day," he said with outstretched arms. Bella sauntered over for a quick pet before moving onto Bode.

"This wind is crazy. Is it going to get worse?" I asked.

"I just came from town. They're expecting the storm this afternoon. Looks like you planned your visit perfectly." He pulled the cooler beside Bode.

"Will you be all right? Grab some coffee," I said.

"Yes, *gracias*, I'll be fine. Ah, yes, I have your mug in the truck. I wanted to return it to you."

"After your coffee," I said.

"*Gracias.*" He stood and walked to the truck to grab the mug and something else—a folded piece of paper. On his way back, he poured himself some coffee. "*Muchacho*, I brought you something," he said, taking a seat on the cooler.

"Jorge—"

He held up a hand.

"It's a traditional Buddhist prayer I keep beside my bed. I thought you might like it so I wrote it down for you. Would you like me to read it to you?"

With his hands in the pocket of his hoodie, Bode nodded. Come to think of it, Bode had had at least one of his hands in his pocket a lot since the other night. At first I thought he was just cold, but that morning I realized that he was clutching the *vajra*.

Jorge glanced at me, as if seeking permission to read the prayer to Bode.

I nodded, and as he cleared his throat to begin, I laughed, thinking it was a bit too late to ask for my approval.

Jorge read slowly and deliberately, allowing Bode to take it in. "May all beings have happiness and the causes of happiness. May all beings be free from suffering and the causes of suffering. May all beings never be parted from freedom's true joy. May all beings dwell in equanimity, free from attachment and aversion."

Bode sat pensively before asking what "equimity" meant.

"Composure," I said. "Calmness."

"Do you like it?" Jorge asked.

Bode nodded. "I 'specially like the part about all beings being free from suffering."

"*Es*pecially," I corrected, though I wondered if *specially* was also correct.

"I made this copy for you," Jorge said, folding the paper and handing it to Bode.

"Thank you, *Señor Espinoza*," Bode said and stood to hug Jorge.

I prepared a feast for breakfast using most of what was left in the cooler. With the blustering wind, I was grateful for having the new grill I picked up just before the trip, complete with side shelves that doubled as wind-blockers. Bode brought over a few plates, and I served three monster portions of scrambled cheese eggs and home fries. Pleased with my creation, I filled my mug with more coffee and joined Bode and Jorge beside the fire.

We ate quickly, stuffing our faces before the wind could pick up any more steam and throw sand in our food. I asked Jorge if he was confident with the tablet and whether he had any questions. He said it was intuitive enough and would email me if he had any questions, as if he'd been emailing for years. He said he, in fact, had already sent me one email.

"I like that Pandora application you installed," he said.

"It's one of my favorites."

"Did you get him *Clash of Clans*?" Bode asked with a string of cheese hanging from his mouth.

"What do *you* think?" I smiled.

Jorge looked at the two of us quizzically.

After relaxing for a few more minutes, we tossed our plates into the fire and watched them fold and turn black. Bode asked if it was okay to sit atop the bluff for a bit, presumably to meditate, and I said of course. Jorge smiled and watched as Bode and Bella ambled to the overlook.

"He's a good boy, Matthew."

"Thanks, Jorge. I'm glad you were finally able to meet him. It's been too long. But now that you have the tablet, you'll have to Facetime us."

"I can't thank you enough."

"It's my pleasure. I'm just glad you'll be able to see Ana and Pablo after so long."

"Ana and Pablo are happy, thanks to you and your—"

"Complete disregard for U.S. immigration law," I mocked in unison. "I know, you remind me every time."

"Well, because of you they are happy and living the American Dream."

"I'm not sure there is such a thing anymore, but I'm glad they're happy. I just wish you were able to be with them."

Jorge gave an encouraging smile, but I sensed sadness hidden beneath. It reminded me of a dolphin in captivity, perpetually smiling but unable to express its true emotions. I respected him for the compassion he showed his wife and son, and the sacrifice he had made to ensure their happiness, despite losing the two most meaningful things in his life. Perhaps that's what made it bearable for him—by caring more about their welfare than his own, he was able to let go. I wasn't sure I would have been able to make such a sacrifice.

I rose to my feet and lifted my arms. Jorge stood and accepted my embrace.

"It was so good seeing you, Jorge. Thank you for everything."

"*Mi amigo*, I did nothing. Thank you for visiting me. And thank you for bringing your boy. It was an honor to have met him."

I carried the dishes to the beach to rinse them off in the ocean. When I returned, Jorge had already packed the E-Z Up in its box for me and set it beside the truck. I packed the dishes in the bins along with the mugs, fire starter, headlamps, and other miscellaneous gear we had scattered around the site.

By the time Bode was finished meditating, I had the back of the truck packed tight with easy access to our duffel bag, shoes, and CamelBaks. I felt as if I was forgetting something but that was normal after having all your possessions scattered for days. Jorge kneeled down and spoke softly to Bode while I started the car. When I returned to the back of the truck, the two were hugging and Bode was nodding into Jorge's shoulder. After a long embrace, Jorge stood and gave me a hug goodbye.

Bode climbed into his booster seat and Jorge walked me to the driver's side door. For the first time I noticed his fingers, old and wrinkled, yet stronger and more capable than my own. At that moment, I realized that I loved this man like the father I had lost long ago.

"Take care of that boy, Matthew."

I put my hand on his. "Be well, old man. We'll Facetime you when we get home."

Jorge leaned forward to get a last look at Bode and said, "Remember what I told you, *muchacho*. And a safe journey to you both."

The same man was working at the service station in Eréndira and kindly attended to the tires. I thanked him for his help and tipped him another five dollars. We made one final stop—a couple burritos for the road—before heading north. As I started the truck, I looked up at Bode in the rearview and asked him what Jorge had told him before we'd hopped in the car.

"He said to follow my thoughts only when they were in

harmony with my heart."

"That's good advice. Do you understand what it means?"

Bode nodded.

I smiled at him in the mirror, put the truck in gear, and left a dust cloud as I pulled out of the driveway and onto the paved road.

fourteen

WITH THE MEMORY OF the masked gunmen still fresh in my mind, it was impossible for me to relax for the duration of the drive. Fortunately, other than the increasingly forceful winds, the journey was uneventful and the two checkpoints we encountered along the way were legitimate and manned by the Mexican Federal Police.

As we approached the exit for Ensenada, I asked Bode if he needed a rest. He shook his head and I pressed down on the accelerator, continuing north on Mexico 1 toward Tijuana. We made good time and reached the outskirts of TJ shortly after noon. It's not uncommon to wait several hours to cross into the States, and I was pleased to make it to the back of the line before one o'clock.

Beneath the ashen sky of Tijuana we sat, queued up for nearly two hours, inching forward. It seemed as if the sky was sapphire blue just beyond the border. In all my years traveling to Mexico, I don't think it had ever been sunny in Tijuana, which was surprising considering both San Diego and Punta Cabras both enjoyed three hundred days of sunshine per year.

As the minutes passed, I was kicking myself for not stopping in Ensenada to use the restroom. We passed the time by pointing out all the items for sale on the side of the road: T-shirts, soccer jerseys from nearly every Latin American country, Mexican *Falsa* and *Serape Saltillo* blankets, and every other knickknack and tchotchke you could imagine. I bought a bag of *churros* from a woman stationed between the lanes of traffic and passed it to Bode.

"What are they?"

"They're like doughnuts. They don't get any better than these."

He said something, but his mouth was stuffed and I couldn't make it out.

"They're delicious, right? They're even better dipped in chocolate."

By the time we finished the *churros*, the border was within sight. The painful need to use the restroom had temporarily passed, and I hoped the same was true for Bode. I didn't want to mention it and have him start thinking about it again. We counted the number of vehicles ahead of us and estimated our wait time. With approximately thirty minutes remaining, I suggested we get some more *churros,* and Bode nodded enthusiastically.

The pace of vehicles crossing the border picked up until a hold-up just two vehicles ahead, a white pickup truck, by which time we bouncing in our seats. Five minutes passed, which felt like an absolute eternity, before blue-uniformed officers finally escorted the pickup to a parking area on the right. The car ahead of us passed with no problem and we were finally at the front of the line.

"Passports, please."

I handed the officer my passport along with Bode's birth certificate.

"Does the child have a passport?"

"No, just the birth certificate. And a social security card if that helps," I said, pulling the card from Bode's envelope and handing it to the agent, Officer Calderón.

"Is he your son?"

"Yes."

"Do you have an I-551 card for him?" he asked while inspecting Bode's birth certificate and social security card.

"A what?"

"An I-551 Permanent Resident card."

"No, just his birth certificate and social security card."

"A passport is recommended for all U.S. citizens, including children."

"Is the birth certificate and social security card not sufficient? Clearly, he's my son—he has the same last name." I was growing frustrated.

"Do you have a notarized letter signed by his mother authorizing travel to and from the country?"

"His mother is deceased."

The agent looked at me in the eye for the first time. "Do you have a copy of her death certificate?"

"Holy shit, are you serious?"

"Dad."

"Sir?"

"I do." I reached into the glove compartment and pulled out the other two envelopes labeled *Eliza* and *Sophie*. I opened the envelope labeled *Eliza* and pulled out the Certification of Death and handed it to the officer.

"What's the other envelope?" he asked as he unfolded Eliza's death certificate.

"Our dead dog's vaccination history. Would you like that, too?"

"Sir, please watch your tone."

"We've been waiting in line for more than two hours, we're about to piss ourselves, and you're giving us the third degree."

"Sir, please calm down."

I took a deep breath and waited.

"It says that Mrs. Eliza Price died December 30, 2017, and this child was born just a few days earlier. Do I have that correct?"

"Yes, you have that correct. Must we have this discussion?" I said and nodded in Bode's direction.

"We can have this discussion inside," Calderón threatened.

"Is there a pisser?"

"Sir?"

"Nothing," I said. "Perhaps you can radio for Officer Rodriguez?"

"Who?"

"Officer Rodriguez. We were stopped last week crossing the border and a Mexican patrol officer called Officer Rodriguez over when he saw my son in the car."

"You were stopped going *into* Mexico?" Calderón asked as he glanced at a piece of paper taped to the inside of his booth.

"Would you believe that? A father and son getting stopped for no good reason?"

"Don't be facetious, Dad."

I looked up to the rearview and couldn't help but laugh.

"I don't see any Officer Rodriguez, but you've provided sufficient documentation. May I suggest you get your son a passport if you plan on traveling outside of the country."

"Good suggestion," I said and took hold of the documents.

"Welcome home."

I looked at Calderón incredulously and stuffed the papers into their respective envelopes and into the glove compartment. I put the truck in gear and waited for the red and white gate to open. It took every last ounce of restraint to avoid flooring it and leaving Officer Calderón in a cloud of dust.

Minutes later on the 5, Bode said, "That was some good *equimity*, Dad."

I laughed so hard that I nearly drove onto the shoulder. I didn't have the heart to correct him so I just said, "Thanks, buddy. I wanted to rip his head off."

"He wasn't very being very nice. He was—"

"Loathsome? Smug? Condescending?" I said.

"Unhappy."

I looked at him in the rearview and wondered for the billionth time how I had gotten so lucky.

"Hey, Dad?"

"Yeah?"

"Can we stop and pee?"

Fortunately, there was a McDonald's right off Exit 2, so we stopped for a bathroom break, milkshake, and fries. We sat at a table by the window and called Naja to let her know we were back in the States. I passed the phone to Bode so he could say hello. Before handing it back to me, he asked if she wanted to get a dog.

"Seriously? Give me the phone."

Bode smiled and passed it over.

"Sorry about that. No. Well, maybe. We'll talk about it next week."

I told Naja that I wasn't quite sure where we were headed other than generally north for the time being—either toward Los Angeles or Las Vegas. After I hung up, a chime indicated a bunch of new emails, so I let them download while I clicked over to the map.

We had already been in the car for more than five hours, and the thought of driving another five to Las Vegas didn't appeal to either of us. Before leaving the East Coast, I had considered visiting Brett in Santa Monica on the return trip, but as we sat in McDonald's looking at the map, the thought of driving to the west side of L.A. that afternoon only to have to drive through the city the following day wasn't a pleasant one. Perhaps it was my East Coast mentality, but bumper-to-bumper traffic was not something I was prepared for on our cross-country road trip.

In the end, however, we chose Santa Monica. *What's another day*, I thought, so we Facetimed Brett and invited ourselves over. He was thrilled and said he would call Julie to make sure they had nothing happening that night, but reminded me that he had two kids under the age of five; what could be going on? Dinner? A Disney movie? I laughed and motioned for Bode to come over.

"Ready for this?" I said to Brett, pulling Bode onto my lap.

Bode joined me in the camera's viewfinder.

"Whoa, dude! You chopped it off," Brett said. "What a stud. Izzy's going to love you."

"How old is she?" Bode asked.

"She's five. And Isaac is almost one."

"Like me," Bode said eagerly.

"I can't wait to tell them you're coming."

"If there's any problem, just shoot me a text," I said. "We can always stay at a hotel."

"Don't be silly, Julie's going to be psyched you guys are coming. Need directions?"

"No, we're all set."

"When do you think you'll get here? Two, three hours?"

"Yeah, depending on traffic."

"Shouldn't be too bad, it's Saturday."

"It is?" I looked at Bode who just shrugged. "Okay, we'll see you around five or so. Text me if we should aim for a hotel."

"Stop it, we'll see you soon. See you later, Bodeman!"

I clicked over to email to find twenty-four emails, which wasn't too bad after four days off the grid. I scrolled through the list of senders and noticed two from Jorge. I smiled at the thought of receiving email from my friend who—until a day ago—*lived* off the grid. I tapped on the first, sent yesterday:

> **From:** Jorge Espinoza
> <puntacabras@gmail.com>
> **Date:** August 18, 2023 7:21:09 AM PST
> **To:** Matthew Price
> <matthewprice@me.com>
> **Subject:** Test
>
> It's a real pain writing on this *cochinada*.
>
> Jorge

"What'd he write?" Bode asked.

"He said it's a pain in the butt to type on the tablet."

We laughed and I tapped on his second email, sent just a couple hours ago:

> **From:** Jorge Espinoza
> <puntacabras@gmail.com>
> **Date:** August 19, 2023 10:21:22 AM PST
> **To:** Matthew Price
> <matthewprice@me.com>
> **Subject:** Safe journey
>
> Matthew,

By the time you receive this I trust you and
Bode will be safely across the border. Thank
you for visiting me. I had a wonderful time
with you both. Bode is a special boy. I look
forward to staying in touch with you.
Matthew, I cannot tell how you grateful I
am for everything you have done for me and
my family.

Muchas gracias,
Jorge

I tapped reply.

From: Matthew Price
<matthewprice@me.com>
Date: August 19, 2023 2:04:09 PM PST
To: Jorge Espinoza
<puntacabras@gmail.com>
Subject: Re: Safe journey

Hi Jorge! It was great seeing you as well.
Bode and I had a great time, too. We just
made it over the border and pulled over for
a quick rest. We've decided to head north to
visit Brett in L.A. Speak to you soon!

Matthew

P.S. I hope you are weathering the storm—I
think we outran it!

I scanned the rest of the messages while Bode worked on his
shake. One email caught my attention. It was from my future

boss, Ashton Barcott, the president of 4.0, welcoming me to the agency. His tone sounded a bit formal, I noted, as he expressed his enthusiasm about me joining the team. I looked at the email header and noticed that he cc:ed a few of the other senior members of the team. I tapped reply and thanked him for his note, saying we had just crossed the border, and I would drop him a line when we returned home in a week.

I started the truck and programmed Brett's address into the navigation system.

"Two and a half hours to go. You ready?"

Bode responded with a sleepy nod.

The wind was gusting outside but, naturally, the sun had emerged from behind thick white clouds. The dashboard read seventy-four degrees and I opened the sunroof as I pulled out of the parking lot. When I merged back onto the 5, I looked in the rearview and found Bode doubled over. How he could sleep like that I'll never understand. I set the cruise control to seventy-five, plugged in the phone, and fired up the *Long Haul* playlist.

After a few minutes, I heard a chime and looked at the phone: seven new voicemails. I plugged in my earpiece and turned the volume down on the radio. I listened to the messages: a couple friends saying hello; Eliza's mother, Anne; Barcott checking to see if I had received his email; Naja calling to see if we were back in the States. The voicemails were bookended by two messages from my father's brother, Michael.

Uncle Michael was twelve years younger than my father and was more like an older cousin than an uncle. He was about fifty, a couple years older than my father had been when he died. Uncle Michael sounded a little concerned on his second message since he hadn't heard back from me in several days. I called him to put him at ease and pass some time. Michael was a nice guy, though I didn't really know him too well. I hadn't seen him since my wedding and only a handful of times before that. He seemed genuinely interested in our cross-country adventure and asked how Bode slept in a tent. "As well as he does in his bed, the lucky dog," I laughed. Michael said that I shouldn't be a stranger and then invited us to visit him and Aunt Mary in Columbus on our way home. I told him we had just figured out today's plan, but I would give him a ring if our journey east took us through Ohio.

When I ended the call, I felt grateful for people like Michael. It was nice to know there was at least one family member who cared about Bode and me, no matter the distance—emotionally or geographically—that separated us from them. Our family was so small and Bode didn't have a sibling or even one first cousin. To make matters worse, he hardly ever saw his Grandmother Anne whom, short of actually coming out and saying anything, seemed to harbor ill feelings for us ever since Eliza's death.

A wave of sadness washed over me. While I was supposed to be growing the family, death seemed more prevalent than life. I wondered what Bode made of it all. Without anything to compare it to, I wondered if he took notice that his family was pretty much as small as it gets. Did that make him sad? Was he afraid of death? Or my death? Did he even think about it?

The voice from the navigation system brought me back into the truck. *That was a quick hour*, I thought. Bode stirred in the back when I merged onto 73 but remained asleep.

Bode knew my parents died when I was just a teenager, but thankfully he hadn't yet asked for details. I did not look forward to telling him about the night in which one family lost their sixteen-year-old boy while another sixteen-year-old boy lost his family. I knew I would have to explain it one day, but skirting around the details of his mother's death was hard enough.

"What are you thinking about?"

"You don't know?" I said, glancing at him in the rearview and smiling. "I thought you were sleeping."

"I was. You were thinking about something sad."

"Yeah, just stuff. How was your nap?"

"Okay."

"We'll be there in an hour or so. Do you need to stop?"

"Nah."

I reached back and grabbed his foot. "I love you, buddy."

Traffic slowed, and I opened the windows to get some air.

"So, what were you thinking about?" Bode said.

"You really want to know?" I asked, looking up to the rearview and stalling.

He nodded.

"Let me ask you something," I said, uncertain whether I wanted to tell him exactly what was on my mind. "Are you afraid of anything?"

Bode thought for a moment as he looked out the window. "Nothing I can think of," he finally said.

"Are you afraid of the dark?"

"No."

"What about monsters?"

"Dad, you're being silly."

I smiled and turned the radio up a bit.

After a minute, Bode said, "I guess I'm afraid of becoming like them."

"Like whom?" I said, turning the volume back down.

"Like all those people," he said, gesturing to the cars and trucks around us. "Most of them look sad."

"What do you mean?" I asked.

"They just look sad. I wonder what they are so sad about."

"Maybe they're just thinking about stuff. You know, to pass the time."

"What were you thinking about?"

I wanted to punch myself for setting myself up like that. "Grandma and Grandpa."

"Oh." After several seconds he asked, "Do you miss them?"

"Sometimes. It's been a long time. I talk to them once in a while though."

"Like we talk to Mom?"

"Yeah, but it's much easier to speak to Mom because I knew her so well. I know what she's going to say when I talk to her. It's just gotten harder with my parents because I don't have too many memories of them."

He understood. All he had of his own mom were stories I had shared with him. But those didn't constitute memories, did they? Memories or no memories, Bode was going to remember his mother as the woman she was—beautiful, strong, determined, silly and adventurous. Fortunately, all of those qualities were unmistakably part of Bode and for that I was grateful. We would often talk about Eliza, and I'd impart details about who she was and what she would have done or said. I'd share stories with him that demonstrated her compassion or emphasized her courage and determination. I'd tell him that her favorite color was blue, that she had an insatiable sweet tooth and, much to his amusement, how she embraced every opportunity to don a costume. I would tell him that thunderstorms were the only thing that truly frightened her but they scared her like he wouldn't believe. I explained how she had horrible taste in movies but excellent taste in literature. I would tell him how accomplished she was at work, yet she never let it define who she was. As the youngest partner at her crisis management consulting firm, Eliza was as calm under pressure as they come, and she could weather the most tempestuous of storms in the boardroom.

"Did Mom believe in heaven?"

"What makes you ask that?" I said, wondering where he would have learned about heaven in the first place.

Bode just shrugged.

Traffic finally opened up, and I closed the sunroof so we could hear one another.

"I'm not sure. She never really mentioned it. She wasn't afraid, if that's what you're asking."

A slight smile appeared on his face.

"You're not afraid, are you?" I said.

He looked at me in the mirror.

"Of death, I mean. You're not afraid, are you?"

"Why should I be?"

"You shouldn't. I used to think about it a lot after my parents died," I continued, looking for clues to see if he ever considered it. "In college, I read a really funny quote by Mark Twain."

"Who?"

"Mark Twain. He was a famous author. You'll read some of his books in a few years. You know what he said about death?"

"What?"

"He said, 'I don't fear death. I had been dead for billions and billions of years before I was born, and I had not suffered the slightest inconvenience from it.' Isn't that funny?"

Bode smiled and nodded.

"I mean, once you're dead, what's there to worry about? I worry about leaving you behind, but that's it. It's actually my only fear. Leaving you."

"You're not afraid of thunderstorms?"

"I love them," I laughed. "Except when we're camping."

"What about sailing?"

I looked up to the rearview and smiled. "Okay, that, too."

"Did Mom like Jorge?"

"A lot. After Brett and Julie's wedding your mom and I drove down to visit Jorge. She thought he was great. Didn't you?"

Bode nodded. "He is very kind."

I looked up and smiled at his choice of words.

Several minutes passed before either of us spoke again. "Bella's sick," Bode said.

"What?"

"Bella's sick."

"How do you know?"

"She felt the same as Sophie."

"How do you mean?"

Bode shrugged.

"When did you notice?" I asked.

"When you were fishing yesterday."

"Did you say anything to Jorge?"

He shook his head.

"Why not?"

He shrugged. "I didn't want him to make him sad."

We drove in companionable silence the rest of the way to Santa Monica. The GPS was spot on and directed us precisely to Brett and Julie's beige, stucco-finished Spanish-style home, complete with clay-tiled roof and arches over the doorway and windows.

"They *live* here? It looks like a mansion," Bode said.

"I guess so."

Brett and Julie hadn't yet moved to Santa Monica until after they were married and Isabel was on the way. Speaking of Izzy, she spotted the truck as we pulled into the driveway and waited inside, nose pressed against the glass door, as Bode and I grabbed our things. Brett came outside with a bouncing Isabel in tow. We hugged and introduced the kids in person for the first time. Isabel hid behind Brett's leg while Bode took hold of my hand.

"Come on, Bode, it's Brett and Izzy. You see them on Facetime all the time."

Bode looked up at me and smiled.

Brett rubbed Bode's crew cut, already growing in nicely, and picked him up for a hug before inviting us in.

fifteen

THE SHOWER WAS SPECTACULAR. Sure, bathing the previous four days consisted of a dip in the Pacific, but the bathroom reminded me of one at the Four Seasons, complete with L'Occitane soap, plush white bath towels, and fluffy shower rug. I was grateful when Julie showed us to the guest room. Her invitation to freshen up was probably more of a request, but I wasn't going to split hairs. I soaped up a washcloth for Bode and had him shower while I shaved for the first time in nearly a week. Feeling like a new person, I slipped into the last of my clean clothes. Bode wasn't as fortunate so he went commando in his bedtime sweatpants—the only thing not visibly filthy—and one of Izzy's T-shirts. Brett showed us to the laundry and helped us start a load before we joined everyone in the living room.

Julie thought it would be fun for the kids to make their own pizzas. Bode was in heaven, making pizza in a household run by a woman. I've never seen a kid eat so many vegetables, and I made a mental note to tell to Naja about it. If Bode was interested in becoming a vegetarian—or simply eating more veggies than I would traditionally serve—I wasn't going to stop him. I mouthed an apology to Julie after Bode attacked the bowl of mushrooms, but she responded with a motherly smile.

After dinner, Julie put Isaac to bed and Bode and Izzy snuggled on the couch in the family room to watch *Toy Story*.

Whether they made it to the end is anyone's guess; we found them passed out on the floor with the DVD back on the title screen. I lifted Bode and carried him to the guest bathroom. By the time I set him on his feet, he was awake enough to do his business. He followed me into the guest room and climbed onto the bed. I tucked him in, told him I would be in soon, but he was already asleep.

I changed the laundry and met Brett and Julie in the living room to continue our assault on the wine cabinet. The conversation turned on me and before I knew it, Brett was probing my romantic life with a sharp instrument, namely his wife. I dodged most of their queries by saying that I'd been too busy at work and spending whatever time I had left with Bode. The main reason for the cross-country trip, I said, was to spend some quality time with the little man since I had been so busy at the office; there simply wasn't any time for women. I should have stopped there. Instead, I added something to the effect of, "And what woman would want a widower with a five-year-old son? It's a lot of baggage."

"Pretty much any woman," she responded energetically, which drew inquisitive looks from Brett and me alike. "You're handsome, successful, a responsible guy, and a great dad. You loved your wife like very few men do and you lost her through God's will."

My eyes drifted to the floor.

"You don't believe in God."

"Not so much," I said, feigning interest in a patch of carpet. Brett shook his head and smiled wryly, knowing where the conversation was headed. On his left was the love of his life, a devout Catholic, and across the coffee table was his agnostic best friend who had been studying Buddhism to try to make sense of it all.

"You lost the love of your life in tragic circumstances," she said in her Southern drawl. It would be one thing if you were divorced with a crazy ex-wife who demanded alimony, fought you for custody, and wanted to boil the bunnies of anyone who got near you. That might be considered baggage, but even then, you're a good looking, successful guy with a beautiful son. You've got everything women want."

Religious debate averted, Brett breathed a sigh of relief into his wine glass.

"Thank you," I said. "It's just hard to think about women when I've got so much on my plate, you know? I don't have the time, and I'm not sure I have the heart to work on a relationship."

"I'm not suggesting you should *do* anything. I'm simply suggesting you be open to it."

"Yeah, don't go joining eHarmony or anything," Brett added.

I smiled at him and finished my wine.

The conversation remained lighthearted for the remainder of the evening. Julie spoke of a few of her friends with whom she would love to set me up. We listened as Brett critiqued each of them and laughed until our heads ached. The wine had won the battle and we retired to bed around midnight.

Bode and I woke to the sound of pans clanking against the stove and the table being set. The aroma of fresh coffee found its way into our room and I cuddled with Bode for a few more minutes before we got up.

"I dreamed about Mom," Bode whispered.

"You did?" *Was that possible?*

"She said she loved me."

"That makes sense," I said.

"She said she loves you, too, and misses us both."

"I miss her."

Bode rubbed his nose. "Dad?"

"Yeah?"

"Do you think you'll ever get married again?"

Had I not just had this conversation just a few hours ago? "I don't know. I don't really think about it too much."

"You don't?"

"Only when you ask me about it," I said and tickled his belly. "Come on, let's get up and help with breakfast." I crawled out of bed.

"Dad?"

"Yeah?"

"You're a good daddy."

"Thanks, buddy. That's sweet of you to say." I walked to Bode's side of the bed and kissed his head. "You're a good boy. Now get your butt in the bathroom and brush your teeth."

Everyone was already awake when we came in. Julie was in the kitchen preparing sausage and pancakes with Isaac, who was in his highchair getting dibs on the first one, while Brett and Izzy were sitting at a dining room table complete with yogurt, blueberries, strawberries, milk and coffee. Bode looked at me as if he had never seen such a spread. I rubbed his crew cut and asked him if he wanted some milk.

"Coffee milk?" he asked.

"I've created a coffee monster," I said.

Izzy observed as I put a few tablespoons of coffee into his milk.

"You want to try it?" Brett asked.

She nodded, so I added a few spoonfuls to her cup.

"Cheers, Mr. Bode," Isabel said and they clinked plastic glasses.

Julie emerged from the kitchen pushing Isaac's highchair to the dining room table. "Isabel, why don't you ask Mr. Bode where he and his dad are going today?"

"Where are you going?"

Bode looked at me and I nodded. "Tell her," I said.

"Las Vegas."

"Las Vegas? What's there?"

Brett and I exchange glances, conjuring up images from my bachelor party.

"Gentlemen," Julie warned.

We laughed and both said, "Sorry."

"The M&M's World," Bode answered.

"Yum!" cried Izzy. "Can we go?"

"Not today but we will one day," Julie promised. She placed a platter of sausage links and pancakes on the table.

"Where are you guys staying?" Brett asked as he served Bode and Isabel pancakes. "The Hard Rock?"

I smiled at him.

"Mr. Brett!"

"Not sure that would be appropriate," I joked. "I haven't actually made a reservation. What do you think? Mandalay Bay? Venetian?" I took the platter and passed it to Julie.

"How about the Bellagio?" Julie suggested. "Bode would love the fountain show."

"That's a good idea," I said. "I think our only requirement is a pool. Right, buddy?"

"With a jacuzzi," Bode added.

"With a jacuzzi. Exactly. I think the Bellagio has one of those."

"Are you being facetious?"

Julie's jaw hit the floor. "That's a big word, Mr. Bode." She turned to me. "That's incredible."

"It's his favorite vocabulary word. There aren't too many others, don't worry," I said to put her at ease. "Izzy, can you tie your shoes?"

She nodded proudly.

"Yeah? How 'bout you, little man?"

Bode smiled and shook his head, proof that Julie's daughter was just fine.

"Yes, but the fact that he was able to detect the tone of your voice."

"What?" Bode, asked. "He was being *sartastic*."

"Sarcastic," I corrected. "That's another."

Julie was beside herself. "Miss Isabel, we've got some work to do."

After clearing the table, I folded our laundry and packed our duffle bag, leaving out an outfit for Bode. I let him play with Isabel while I took a quick shower and got dressed. Afterward, I sat with Brett on the couch in the family room while Izzy taught Bode how to play Wii tennis. Brett was reading *The New York Times* on his tablet, tapping and dragging and pinching away.

"What's new in the world?" I asked.

"Same old stuff. There's an interesting Op-Ed piece by Thomas Friedman about how the environment is going to shit—"

"Dad!" cried Izzy.

"—and how the wealthiest two percent of the planet is to blame."

"That makes sense."

Brett placed the tablet on the couch and got up to refill his coffee mug.

"Bode, we're going to take off soon. We've got about five hours of pavement ahead of us. Let's get dressed after this game, okay?"

"O—kay," he grunted as he nailed a crosscourt winner with his backhand.

Half an hour later we were thanking Brett and Julie for their hospitality and saying our goodbyes on the front lawn.

I lifted Izzy for a hug. "We'll see you on the computer when we get home, okay?" I said.

Izzy nodded and gave me a kiss on the cheek. I set her down and gave Julie a hug. Holding Isaac in his arms, Brett walked Bode and me to the truck. I gave him half a hug, careful not to crush Isaac, and affectionately rubbed the little man's head. Brett closed my door after I'd climbed into the truck and walked around to Bode's side. I opened his window, but Brett had already opened the door.

"I want a hug," Brett said and carefully leaned in without banging Isaac's head.

Bode gave Brett a big hug and said goodbye to Isaac.

Brett and the girls waved goodbye from the front lawn as we pulled out of the driveway and down the palm tree-lined street.

In no time, we were on I-10 heading east, but I mistakenly got on 405 North. Though we ended up taking the long way through Los Angeles, it provided Bode the opportunity to catch a glimpse of the HOLLYWOOD sign from the 101 and I was happy to share a bit of trivia that I had picked up while pledging my fraternity at USC. The sign was originally constructed in 1923 and read "HOLLYWOODLAND." It was only designed to be up for a year or two but it had remained ever since.

"What happened to the other letters?" Bode asked.

Bode couldn't read many words yet, and I wondered if I had said anything to suggest it didn't still say "HOOLYWOODLAND." I assumed he figured it out because I had already called it "the HOLLYWOOD sign."

"Well, there are rumors that the last four letters, the L-A-N-D, fell down in 1949, but the truth is they were taken down deliberately as part of a makeover. How tall do you think they are?" I asked, recalling my pledge brother who had to chug a beer because he didn't remember.

"A hundred feet?" Bode guessed.

"Not quite," I said. "Forty-five. And they're thirty-one to thirty-nine feet wide."

That didn't seem to impress Bode, though he continued to stare in the sign's direction long after it was out of sight.

"And that's where Daddy went to school," I said, pointing to the right.

"USC," he said.

"That's right. I haven't been back in a long time but it's a couple miles that way."

"Where am I going to go to college?"

"Anywhere you want. But let's get through first grade, huh? You're growing up too fast. Did you grow again last night?" He nodded proudly. "Well, slow down. Slow down!"

Traffic was light and we appeared to be making good time. I called back to Bode, "Three and a half hours to go. I figure we'll stop at In-N-Out for a quick rest and book a hotel?"

"And a shake?"

"If that's what you'd like," I said. "We'll be there in an hour. Want the phone?"

Bode shook his head and fixated on the increasingly rugged landscape as we continued toward the San Bernardino National Forest. The terrain began to flatten out and gave way to a more desert-like appearance as we headed toward Hesperia, Victorville, and other towns I could not seem to recall ever passing during my college Vegas trips.

In-N-Out Burger in Barstow was exactly as I remembered. While we weren't necessarily hungry after the breakfast spread at Brett and Julie's, how could a person enjoy fries and a shake at In-N-Out Burger without indulging in a Double-Double? I convinced Bode to order a grilled cheese as well, suggesting he could always take it with him if he wasn't hungry. While waiting for our order, I fired up the Hotels.com app to check out room rates in Las Vegas. I was afraid the rate for the Bellagio would be incredibly expensive but that turned out not to be the case. After all, it was a Sunday in August, the hottest month of the year.

Our number was called, and I sent Bode to retrieve the tray from the counter as I booked a room. I hadn't yet told Bode, but I thought it would be fun to camp for a night at the Grand Canyon. Earlier, while he was getting schooled in Wii Tennis, I had mapped Las Vegas to Westport on Brett's tablet. The suggested route would have taken us through Utah, Colorado and Nebraska, but the North Rim of the Grand Canyon would have been more than three hours off-route. I dragged the suggested route south to check out the South Rim of the Canyon and found the hour and half diversion from I-40 to be much more palatable. The route from Flagstaff east would take us through New Mexico, the Texas panhandle, and Oklahoma before angling northeast toward the Midwest.

"I wish we had our chess set," Bode said when he returned with the food.

"You know, I was thinking about that earlier. Maybe we can pick one up." I stole a fry as he set down the tray.

A light colored golden retriever was lying in the shade outside the restaurant when we walked outside. It wasn't tied up but it lay obediently beside an In-N-Out Burger French fry tray filled with water. Its coat had been trimmed recently, and it looked more like a yellow Lab, though its floppy ears were a dead giveaway. Bode kneeled to pet the animal.

"Look," Bode said. "Her name is Sophie."

At first, I wondered how he knew, but then I noticed the large black letters on the green collar along with an 818 phone number.

"A valley dog," I said.

"A what?"

"A valley dog. Eight one eight is the area code for the valley outside L.A. Looks like Sophie's on a road trip herself."

"Maybe she's going to Las Vegas, too."

"Maybe, but I can't imagine Las Vegas being much fun for a dog." And then I wondered if I had ever seen a dog in Las Vegas in all my visits.

"You know what that means?" I said as we walked to the truck. "Las Vegas?"

"What?"

"*The meadows.*"

That didn't seem to impress Bode, and he climbed into his seat without comment.

"In the 1800s, it was a stopping point for water for travelers headed to Southern California."

Crickets. Clearly he didn't share my enthusiasm for useless trivia. *Just like his mother.*

By the time we reached Las Vegas, the temperature had climbed to ninety-two degrees and showed no sign of slowing down. I was hoping to show Bode the *Welcome to Fabulous Las Vegas Nevada* sign, but the navigation system took us straight to E. Flamingo Road. At the red light before turning onto Las Vegas Boulevard, I turned around to look at Bode. His mouth was agape and his eyes wide.

"Crazy, huh?"

He could only nod.

"Just wait." The light turned green and I turned right on the Boulevard. "Do you know what that is?" I asked, pointing to the left.

"Uh-uh."

"It's the Eiffel Tower. Well, a replica. The real one is in Paris, and it's twice the size. An engineer named Gustave Eiffel designed it for the World's Fair in Paris."

I looked to the rearview and saw Bode staring out his window. A fountain show in front of the Bellagio was in progress, sending hundreds of streams of water into the sky in sync with music—"Luck Be A Lady," was it? I turned off the radio and opened the windows so Frank Sinatra could dance into the truck. I made another right onto W. Bellagio Drive and drove slowly, sneaking peeks at Bode in the rearview. I silently gave thanks to Julie for an excellent recommendation.

While checking in at the front desk, I received an email from Jorge. I tapped on it while the woman banged away on her keyboard.

From: Jorge Espinoza
<puntacabras@gmail.com>
Date: August 20, 2023 2:34:11 PM PST
To: Matthew Price
<matthewprice@me.com>
Subject: Question

Except for the subject, the email was empty. I figured I had a bad signal and the remainder of the email would download momentarily, so I slid the phone into my pocket. The woman placed our room keys along with a map of the property on the marble counter in front of me. She pointed over my left shoulder and said, "Your room is straight that way, to the right, past the first elevator bank, stay to the right and you'll take the second set of elevators on your left."

I must have stared at her blankly.

"Sir?"

"Sorry, what's the room number again?"

"1211."

"Thanks, I'm sure we'll find it," I said, pulling the duffle over my shoulder. "You ready?"

It took us about ten minutes, but we finally made it to what I believed was the correct elevator bank. Funny thing was, we'd walked a relatively straight line despite the woman's complicated directions.

Bode was speechless.

"A little crazy?" I said as we stepped into the elevator.

He nodded. I placed a hand on his head and smiled at him in the closing mirrored doors. At the last moment, a hand appeared and the doors bounced open. A man and a woman entered. So cliché, I thought: a silver haired man dressed to the nines with a piece of candy on his arm. The man, old enough to be my father—and actually resembling what he might have looked like if my dad wore $2,000 suits—gave me a nod like his party was all accounted for, and would I please press the "close doors" button. The woman flashed huge teeth and said, "Hi, sweetie pie!" to Bode in a Southern meets Midwest meets Waffle House accent.

Do women still wear sequins?

Bode's cheek twitched a half smile and he looked to the elevator floor. His hands were fidgeting in the pocket of his hoodie.

"What floor?" I asked.

He reached over and slid his room key into the slot beside the numbers and pressed thirty-six. Of course. The elevator rose directly to the twelfth floor and when the doors opened, I guided Bode forward, nodding to the couple.

"Dad?"

"Yeah, buddy?"

"How long are we staying here?" he asked, rubbing his temple.

"We'll leave first thing," I assured him. "Grab breakfast and hit the road early."

As we navigated the hallway, I wondered whether the stimulation of the town was distressing him. Surely he couldn't be aware of the lost fortunes, debauchery and seedy reputation of the city.

"What are you thinking?"

"Nothing."

We stopped at room 1211 and I looked at him before sliding the key in the door. "Okay, what are you *feeling*?"

He looked at me and smiled.

"Well?" I said as I opened the door.

"I don't know. A little weird, I guess."

We walked into a beautiful room with two double beds. I set the duffle between the two and sat at the foot of the first bed.

"Describe it," I said, patting the bedspread beside me.

Bode sat and looked at his feet, toes barely touching the carpet.

"Talk to me, buddy."

"You know when you touch your tongue to a battery?"

"A nine-volt?" I asked.

He nodded and smiled, remembering the time I tricked him into doing it. I wasn't really tricking him, of course. I was just teaching him how to tell if the battery was dead, like any good father would do.

"Well, it kind of feels like that. Just all over."

"*Really?*" My body tingled at the thought of it. "So, you actually feel the energy?" I had heard about EMFs—electromagnetic frequencies—and how we're exposed to something like a hundred thousand times as much as our grandparents. I started to wonder if Bode was somehow able to sense the city's incessant energy physically.

He nodded.

"When did it start?" I put my arm around him and took hold of his little thigh.

"In the lobby," he said. "It's like when the little hairs on my arms stand up when I'm cold. They don't, I looked, but that's what it feels like. But all over."

"Are you uncomfortable?" I asked.

"Not really. It's only uncomfortable when I feel like that for a while."

"When else do you feel like that?" I was curious to know where else he might feel energy like Las Vegas—and whether it was closer to home and less expensive to visit, I joked to myself.

"I don't know. It's not something I think about after the feeling goes away. Sometimes at the mall, I guess. You know those little tent thingies that sell mobile phones?"

"The kiosks, you mean?"

"Every time I pass one of those I feel kind of weird. There's also a traffic light that takes forever on the way home from school."

"On the Post Road?" I guessed.

He nodded. "Naja and I laugh all the time because we never make that light. We start talking about it from the light before because it's green forever until we get close, but then it turns red."

"I think I know the light you're talking about. Near Winslow Park?"

"There's something about that . . ."

"Intersection."

He nodded. "I feel it there, too."

"Really? Have you said something to Naja?"

"No. What am I supposed to say? 'Naja, I feel like I just licked a battery?'"

"Ha!" I said and then I laughed even harder when he started laughing at his own joke. "You're funny."

"Do you think I'm being silly?"

"About how you feel the energy of things? Not at all." I pulled him close. "Is it like when you felt the energy of the mussels? Or Bella?"

"Not really. I only feel the energy in my hand then."

"That's really cool," I said.

"You can't do it?"

"I don't think so. I've never tried, but I don't think I could."

"I bet you could." He also thought I could fight off evil and leap tall buildings in a single bound. If he stopped to consider it, he would probably think I was going to singlehandedly win the Unilever account from my former company.

"Do you want to get out of here? I mean the room. We're here for the night but do you want to get out of here for a while? We can take a walk to the M&M's World."

"Okay."

I pulled him to my lap for a hug. He wrapped his arms around my neck and my heart sang.

"Hey buddy, will you tell me when you feel stuff in the

future? I hope you'll teach me more about it."

"Okay."

I placed a hand on his back and we stood. "Should we run through the lobby? We can race. Take this hoodie off, though. It's super hot out," I said. "You can put the *vajra* in your shorts."

He looked at me like I had X-ray vision.

I pulled out the phone to see if the M&M's World was within walking distance and noticed another email from Jorge.

> **From:** Jorge Espinoza
> <puntacabras@gmail.com>
> **Date:** August 20, 2023 2:46:05 PM PST
> **To:** Matthew Price
> <matthewprice@me.com>
> **Subject:** Question
>
> Sorry, I pressed send by mistake earlier. When you were fishing the other day, Bode mentioned he was born beneath a tree in front of your house. Is that true? I only ask because I was just reading about the original Buddha and he was also born under a tree while his mother was en route to her family's village. Sadly, his mother also died a few days after childbirth. Strange coincidence, don't you think?
>
> Jorge

I tapped reply.

> **From:** Matthew Price
> <matthewprice@me.com>

Date: August 20, 2023 3:11:23 PM PST
To: Jorge Espinoza
<puntacabras@gmail.com>
Subject: Re: Question

True story. Scariest day of my life. That is
strange! Hope you're well, old man. We're
in Las Vegas for the night. Off to the Grand
Canyon tomorrow so we might be without
service for a bit. Tell Bella that Bode misses
her!

It was scorching outside, and I was glad I'd thought to take
some bottled water. According to the phone, the M&M's World
was only a mile down Las Vegas Boulevard, though it was nearly
half a mile through the lobby and down West Bellagio Drive
itself. Under normal circumstances, a couple of miles was
nothing, even for Bode's little legs, but with the temperature
hovering around the century mark, it was a challenge just to put
one foot in front of the other. Bode walked on my left and
watched the fountains dance to Celine Dion's "My Heart Will
Go On." There was a gentle breeze coming off the eight-acre lake
but it felt as pleasant as a T-Rex wheezing in your face. We
turned right onto the boulevard and I asked Bode how he was
doing.

"Fine," he said. "It's hot here."

"It sure is. The Meadows, my butt," I said, and Bode giggled.

"Hey, we have that at home," he said, pointing to one of the
restaurants.

"That's right."

"P-f . . ." he was sounding it out. "P.F. Chang's, right?"

"You got it. Good reading."

"I just remembered the name of it," he conceded with a smile.

Despite the Las Vegas Convention and Visitors Authority's best effort to promote it as a kid-friendly destination, Las Vegas would never have been shortlisted as a place I longed to take my son had it not been on the way (*in* the way) to somewhere else. I recalled my first visit to the city with my freshman year girlfriend and how we had ducked into the M&M's World to cool off in their A/C. Since that had been the only kid-friendly place I'd visited in all previous trips, it was the only place I mentioned to Bode when the idea of stopping in Las Vegas arose.

According to its website, the M&M's World was a 28,000 square-foot, four-story structure, like "walking up to chocolate heaven." Bode certainly felt the energy; we were just one step inside the door when he turned and asked why we were there.

"What do you mean?" I asked. "I thought you wanted to come here."

Bode shrugged.

"Wanna keep walking?"

He nodded.

Out on the street, I took Bode's hand.

"I don't really like chocolate, you know."

"You must be one of about six kids in the entire world who doesn't," I laughed and squeezed his hand. "Was it too crowded?"

He nodded and asked if we could go back to the hotel and swim, maybe catch another fountain show. We crossed the street and headed back to the hotel, stopping briefly for some water. The fountain display was between shows so we changed into our bathing suits and hit the pool for a couple hours. Bode wanted to practice his swimming so I guided him into the deep end and back. After a few laps I took a break in a shady lounge chair while he swam in the shallow end. I pulled out my phone to check the news and spotted another new message from Jorge:

> **From:** Jorge Espinoza
> \<puntacabras@gmail.com\>
> **Date:** August 20, 2023 3:26:44 PM PST
> **To:** Matthew Price
> \<matthewprice@me.com\>
> **Subject:** Birthday
>
> When was Bode born?
>
> Jorge

I tapped reply.

> **From:** Matthew Price
> \<matthewprice@me.com\>
> **Date:** August 20, 2023 3:32:20 PM PST
> **To:** Jorge Espinoza
> \<puntacabras@gmail.com\>
> **Subject:** Re: Birthday
>
> December 23, 2017. Why, does he share a
> birthday with Buddha, too? :)

After pressing send, I noticed the battery was already low and wondered how that had happened. I put it on standby. Looking up, I saw Bode sitting on the top stair of the pool. I couldn't tell if his eyes were closed, but I imagined they were. Instead of calling over to him, I walked around the pool and, sure enough, they were. I sat in a poolside chair and observed him. A woman and a boy about Bode's age entered the pool. They were holding hands, the boy one step ahead of his mother. As he descended the stairs, he turned toward Bode and slowed, confused at the sight of a boy with his eyes closed sitting on the pool's stairs. His mother put a hand on her son's shoulder and nudged him forward, also stealing a glance at Bode before wading into the pool behind her son. She turned to look for Bode's guardian and after cycling through a few facial expressions that I interpreted as interest and confusion and concern, she finally made eye contact with me, and I smiled to put her at ease. I walked back to my original lounge chair and sat down.

I pressed the standby button of the phone to see what time it was—after four already—and closed my eyes for a few minutes. I heard Bode take a seat next to me and without opening my eyes asked if he wanted to go upstairs before dinner.

I showered first and soaped up a washcloth for Bode before kicking back on the bed. After putting on his sweatpants and T-shirt, he climbed onto my bed and lay next to me. I put my arm around him and we took a power nap for a couple hours. I woke before Bode and gently reached over him to grab the hotel directory resting on the night table. I flipped open the binder to check out the restaurants in the hotel. Sensi, with its "sustainably grown and naturally raised products" seemed nice, and I called downstairs to make a reservation. Bode stirred as I set the phone down and I asked if he was hungry. He said he was, but we took our time shaking off the cobwebs and getting dressed for dinner.

At the restaurant, I shared my plan for the next couple days, most notably camping out beside the Grand Canyon, which seemed to please Bode. I told him we would pass the Hoover Dam in the morning, but I personally didn't fancy a tour. I didn't tell him that you needed to be eight years old to take the tour, but he agreed that a view of the dam from the highway 1,500 feet downriver was sufficient. He asked what made the dam special, and I told him about its construction in the 1930s.

Bode barely made a dent in the king-sized portion of his Pad Thai noodles, so I helped myself after I'd finished my seaweed salad, chef's special roll, and tuna sashimi. After dinner, we decided to take a walk outside and take in a few fountain shows.

It was still hot, but no longer overbearing. The sky was a deep blue, and the lights of Las Vegas Boulevard kept the town perpetually lit. As we approached the fountains, Bode immediately recognized the "Pink Panther." I struggled to recall the name of the composer as we stood and watched the choreographed water show. I asked Bode to face me for a second and I snapped a few photos of him standing in front of the fountains with the Paris Hotel's Eiffel Tower in the background.

Later in the room, Bode and I lay in the bed closest to the window while he watched TV and I wrote in my journal. I reflected on our trip thus far and felt grateful for the time alone with him. No school, no work, nothing but the two of us. As much as I loved Naja and considered her part of our family, it felt great to spend some quality time alone Bode. When I first considered taking the trip, I'd wondered if I should have invited Naja. I felt bad at first but then figured she would probably enjoy some time to herself anyhow.

Bode's storybook was resting on my stomach, but he fell asleep while watching TV. I turned it off, and he reacted to the newly formed silence by rolling onto his side. My thoughts brought me back to Baja, to Bode surfing the whitewater, and his sense of accomplishment after each wave. I thought about the fish I'd managed to catch and the absurdity of landing it with a beer bottle. I thought about Brett and Julie and the kids, and for the first time recognized a difference between Bode and another child his age, especially during mealtimes. It wasn't that the table was set with plastic utensils and cups for the kids, indicating that Isabel wasn't using proper silverware yet. It wasn't that Isabel used two hands to drink her milk while Bode used just one. After all, she knew how to tie her shoes while Bode still showed no interest in learning. The difference was Bode's awareness. He recognized that there were six of us around the table and the conversation included each of us, including Isaac's baby talk, while Izzy felt the need to be the center of attention. Despite her refined speech, Izzy was still in the "me, me, me" phase. If she wasn't included in the conversation, she would interrupt or do something to steal the spotlight. I thought about the things that Jorge had said and wondered if it was this quality, this sense of awareness, that had prompted him to call Bode remarkable. I smiled at the thought of Jorge spending hours at Coyote Cal's exploring the seemingly infinite universe of the Internet.

I scribbled my ruminations into my journal for another few minutes before it finally came to me—Henry Mancini. I must have laughed aloud because Bode stirred. Henry Mancini composed the theme to the *Pink Panther*. Pleased with myself, I tossed the journal and storybook onto the duffle bag and switched off the light.

sixteen

SUNLIGHT PERMEATED THE ROOM at an ungodly hour, and I kicked myself for not shutting the curtains the night before. I turned toward the window to cuddle with Bode but, of course, he wasn't there. Opening my eyes slowly, I saw him sitting cross-legged on the chair, facing the window between the curtains. If he hadn't been meditating he would have turned around upon hearing me wake, so I crawled out of bed and hit the shower.

It wasn't even seven when I walked back into the room. Bode was dressed and sitting up against the headboard with his storybook on his lap.

"You're reading?" I asked. "Since when?"

"I read with my eyes," he said.

"You mean you read with your memory," I corrected.

He gave me a smirk, knowing he needed to wake up much earlier than seven o'clock in the morning to fool his dad.

"Did you brush your teeth?"

He nodded. "When you were in the shower."

"Really?" I must have been half sleeping, I thought, not to have heard him come in. "Want to grab some breakfast and hit the road?"

The Pool Café wasn't open for another couple hours, so we walked back to The Buffet and were among the first guests to be seated. Bode served himself cereal, yogurt and fruit while I opted for an omelet with bacon and broccoli—the broccoli to make it healthy, I convinced myself. We shared some undercooked, bland home fries from a side plate. If I could make delicious home fries over a campfire, we joked, how could the Bellagio not get it right?

With Las Vegas in the rearview and windows and sunroof open, we drove for about half an hour before reaching Henderson, Nevada. When Bode asked to use the phone, I remembered that it needed a charge. I unplugged the charger from the front and handed it to Bode along with the phone.

"Don't get caught up in a movie," I said. "We'll be passing the Hoover Dam soon. I'll slow down and you'll have to snap a couple pictures."

"Which side will it be on?"

"Not sure." I assumed the left because we would be passing it down river and didn't most rivers run south? That couldn't be true. They run downhill—the path with least resistance—which wasn't necessarily south, like the Santa Cruz River near Picacho Peak. How about in the southern hemisphere, though? I mentally kicked myself for such an airhead moment. Before I answered Bode, I switched the navigation system to map view to see where US-93 crossed the Colorado River. I realized the airhead moment hadn't yet ceased because I still didn't know which direction the river flowed. I vowed to never share this momentary lapse of reason with anyone.

Fortunately, before too long I put two and two together with the assistance of the navigation system. "It'll be on the left," I said after flipping the GPS back onto the written directions. "Want to practice taking a few pictures? Or better yet, you can take a video, and we can take screenshots later."

"Okay."

"You know what you're doing?"

"Click video and push the little button on the bottom."

"You got it," I said. "How's the battery? Still charging?"

"Yep."

After passing through Henderson, the landscape quickly turned rugged with taller mountains looming in the distance beyond Boulder City. It was still early but traffic was already building. After all, it was Monday so people were likely driving to work.

"We're almost at the dam, buddy. Get ready."

Bode unplugged the phone and started tapping buttons.

"I'll drive slowly. Unbuckle and hop over to my side."

In another minute or so, we crossed the Hoover Dam Bypass with the Hoover Dam to the left.

"You getting it?"

"Uh-huh," he said, concentrating on his videography.

I drove over the bridge as slowly as possible and asked him what he thought after the dam was out of sight.

"Okay, I guess."

"Want to go for a tour?" While I'm sure we should have been, neither of us was very impressed and I was content to continue on our way.

"Are you being *sartastic*?"

"I am. Guess what?" I said. "Only two hundred forty-seven miles to go."

"How long is that?"

"About four hours. We'll stop to pick up some food and gas in Kingman," I said, only then realizing we'd crossed into Arizona.

Bode plugged in the phone and set it beside his booster seat. I turned on the radio, and after letting it scan the stations and finding nothing good, handed the auxiliary wire to Bode. When I asked him what he was going to put on, he said John Denver, one of his mom's favorites. Within seconds, "Take Me Home, Country Roads" emerged from the speakers, and I smiled in the rearview. He smiled back and turned toward the window. By the time "Friends With You" began, we were pulling into a Safeway parking lot in Kingman.

We discussed what we were going to cook for dinner as we walked the aisles of Safeway.

"*Cheesadilla*?"

"With vegetables," I insisted.

Finished with our shopping, we emptied the contents of the grocery bags into our cooler along with some fresh ice. We stopped at the Circle K up the street to fill up the tank and use the restroom before hitting the road once again.

I suggested he continue playing DJ, and moments later Jackson Browne's "I'm Alive" filled the truck. I asked if he meant to select Jack Johnson, but he said no, he liked "this guy." I smiled at him in the mirror and turned up the volume.

Outside Kingman, traffic on I-40 became non-existent. More than a quarter mile separated each vehicle, and we cruised with the windows down and Jackson Browne blasting through the speakers. Every now and again I looked to the rearview to check on Bode, who was squinting in the wind and taking in the vista. About a half an hour passed, and we snaked through mountains on either side of us. Once again, the landscape flattened out and it brought back memories of the endless drive through Texas.

The sun climbed high into a cloudless sky but the temperature fortunately remained within a few degrees of eighty as we raced toward Williams, Arizona. Though still very much desert, the landscape surprisingly grew greener and denser along the side of the highway before we turned north. The navigation system said we were less than an hour away from the South Rim and Bode and I grew more and more excited. I had lived in L.A. four years and had visited Las Vegas enough times to make my mother roll in her grave, yet I had never been to the Grand Canyon. For the first time on the trip I felt that sense of wanderlust, the feeling I used to get in my twenties when I would actually take a week off work and travel to new places—London, Paris, Barcelona, Rome, Prague, Reykjavik, Buenos Aires, Rio de Janeiro. Trips I would take before I met Eliza, and then with her, which were more often than not to sailing destinations—Bermuda, Mexico, Hawaii, and the Caribbean. How long had it been, I thought, since I had taken an overnight trip to somewhere other than New Jersey, Ohio, Missouri, or Texas for work?

My backside ached, my legs felt stiff, and I longed to get out of the truck. I asked Bode if he thought we would see a bear and he told me I was being silly. Just then something huge and brown darted across the road and I was forced to slam the brakes.

"What was that? Was that a bear?"

His mouth was wide and his eyes were bugging out of their sockets, an expression that made me break into hysterical laughter. "I don't know," I gasped between cackles, "I think a buck. Did you see the size of its antlers?"

Bode nodded in disbelief. "Maybe there *are* bears around here."

Later at the visitor center, we learned that the animal that dashed across the road was likely a mule deer, very common in those parts. Fortunately, they were much more common than black bear.

I gave the truck some gas and proceeded toward Grand Canyon Village with a bit more caution. We arrived shortly after two and I parked at the Mather Point overlook among more SUVs and motorcycles than I had expected, considering how empty the highway had been. We jumped out of the truck to get our first view of the mile deep canyon. As unimpressive as the Hoover Dam was, the Grand Canyon was simply breathtaking. A vast space surrounded by varied layers of rock ranging in color, composition and depth, innumerable buttes ran the length of the canyon like the spikes and troughs of a seismograph, and side canyons snaked through thousands upon thousands of acres. Even at more than 7,000 feet, we couldn't see the Colorado River a mile below. Bode asked me how far it was to the other side, but it was impossible for me to guess.

We stood awestruck for quite some time before snapping a few photos of the canyon and of one another. At the visitor center, we grabbed a pamphlet with a map of the area and we sat on a bench gathering our bearings, taking note of the Mather campground and the various trails accessible from the South Rim. I suggested we first drive over to the campground to ensure there was a spot for us.

As we walked back to the truck, I continued to scan the pamphlet and spotted some quick facts about the canyon. "It's eight to sixteen miles to the other side," I said, "depending on where you measure."

"Whoa," Bode said, considerably more impressed with the canyon than the Hoover Dam.

We drove to the Mather Campground and secured a campsite. I had little interest in driving around in search of a preferred site so I encouraged the ranger to choose whichever he thought was the best available. We purchased some firewood and headed to our site, which turned out to be fine—fire pit, picnic table, relatively flat ground, and plenty of shade. The table and shade from the surrounding trees were especially welcoming.

After setting up camp, we sat together atop the table and reviewed the map. Trail maps always gave me trouble. No matter how closely I examined one, I always got left and right backward. And elevation? Forget about it. For a while, since I knew I would get it wrong, I started making decisions by choosing the opposite direction of what I determined to be correct. Wouldn't you know, I'd still get it wrong, and more often than not would find myself lost in the woods, save for my phone's GPS.

The pamphlet for the South Rim described various trails, along with distances and estimated durations to certain points along each. We wanted to be back in time to catch the sunset, so we opted for a three-mile hike on the Bright Angel Trail. By the looks of it, the trail seemed to be a straight shot down to the 1½-Mile Resthouse with few opportunities for me to get us lost. This, of course, was appreciated considering I wasn't quite prepared to hike the Grand Canyon in the dark.

"Ready, Hubert?" I asked.

"Hey!"

I rubbed his crew cut, and we hit the trail. Our elevation at the trailhead was 6,850 feet and we would descend about 1,100 feet to the Resthouse. The dirt trail was well maintained and became increasingly steep. The views of the Canyon were spectacular, making it difficult to concentrate on our footing.

We reached the first tunnel after a few minutes and stopped for a few photos. After reaching the first switchback the trail became even steeper and the view even more incredible. Upon reaching the second tunnel, the switchbacks became steeper yet. If I was reading the trail map correctly, we were three quarters of a mile into the hike.

The five-hour drive from Las Vegas was a distant memory,

and I tried to imagine a place I would rather have been than on that hike with my son. Nothing came to mind. However, my thoughts led me to Eliza, and I felt a twinge of sadness. I conjured up her image and initiated a silent dialogue with her, something I had taught Bode to do with his mother and Sophie. I told Eliza that we were doing well and that we talk about her often. *You probably know that*, I said in my thoughts, but I figured I'd say it anyway. I told her about our sailing mishap, and she flashed me a knowing smile. I explained that I was doing my best to interest Bode in sailing but it was so hard without her. *Plus, the kid won't stop climbing things.* As she kissed me on my forehead, I stubbed my foot on a rock and nearly took a spill.

"You okay?" Bode asked.

"I am," I said, laughing at myself.

It was easy to talk to Eliza in the canyon—the vastness, the beauty, the closeness to the collective consciousness. I wondered if Bode was doing the same. Was Eliza having two conversations at once? Was she even paying attention to me? I smiled and skipped to catch up to my son and smacked him on his behind.

"Hey!"

"So, what do you think?"

"It's pretty awesome."

"It is. I'm glad we came. I can't believe I've never been. Maybe one day we'll come back and stay for a while. The pamphlet says the trail goes all the way to the river. You can camp at thirty-eight hundred feet."

"How high are we now?" he asked.

"We started at about sixty-eight hundred." I said between gasps for air. "And we're hiking down to fifty-seven hundred. You think you'd like camping out here for a few nights?"

He said he would.

We walked another fifteen minutes or so and reached the 1½-Mile Resthouse. We took a short break and devoured the granola bars and almonds. After taking a few more photos, we hit the restroom and began the climb to the rim. The pamphlet said to plan twice the amount of time to walk up as it took to walk down. At that rate, I figured we had about two hours of uphill hiking ahead of us. It seemed a bit harrowing, but no matter—onward and upward!

We stopped only for water and to catch our breath. We had taken plenty of photos on the way down and neither of us was in the mood to put on a happy face by the time we reached the first switchback. While balance and stability were required on the way down, it was pure strength needed to get back to the top. Bode was a champ, though, and I rarely doubted his abilities to climb no matter how tired he was. Me on the other hand, I was getting old. By the time we reached the first tunnel, I was happy knowing we had less than a quarter mile to the top.

We high-fived at the rim, and I took a picture of Bode with his arms stretched high overhead. He made me do the same and I felt silly when a couple smiled as they walked by. I told them we just made it from the bottom and their expressions instantly morphed into one of amazement before I told them I was kidding. They laughed and offered to take a picture of the two of us, which I gladly accepted.

Bode and I sat on a bench and considered our options. As I suspected, we didn't have time to eat dinner before the sunset, but we did have time to run back to the site for a few minutes and grab our headlamps. We thought better of walking and took the shuttle to the campground. We changed our shirts and sat at the picnic table for a few minutes while I sucked down a cold Pacifico. I remembered that the South Rim pamphlet mentioned the best places to enjoy a sunset, so we compared its list to the map and agreed on Yaki Point. We grabbed our headlamps and some water and headed over to the visitor center to catch a shuttle.

As if the day could get any more perfect, the sunset was absolutely surreal. If you ever needed to describe the color gold to the blind, the Grand Canyon at sunset would be a fantastic place for inspiration. The entire canyon lit up as if there were a billion tea candles floating on the surface of the Colorado River. Jutting buttes and other formations created shadows throughout the canyon, telling a story of light and shadow with each passing minute. Where the light reached the rock, shades of gold morphed from pale yellow to deep rust depending on the depth and texture of the canyon wall. The sky, once a deep blue with few thin clouds, became red and then purple before finally settling on navy blue. We were only there for a couple hours, but it seemed like an eternity before it actually got dark.

Back at the campsite, we started a fire and set out the ingredients for our quesadillas. My sous chef sat beside me as I sliced the vegetables. We each placed a tortilla on a long piece of foil and piled on our preferred ingredients before sprinkling a generous amount of shredded cheddar onto each. I covered each with a second tortilla, folded over the foil and tossed them onto the fire, which was smoldering at a perfectly low flame. In five minutes, we removed the tortillas and *voila*, dinner was served.

It was probably around ten when we put the fire out and crawled into the tent. We talked about catching the sunrise if we woke in time, but I had a pretty good feeling that sunrise was at five or six and we wouldn't make it. Instead of a story, Bode asked me to read the poem that Jorge had given him. He handed me the poem and I held the poem up in front of our faces as we lay on our backs. The light from the hanging lamp shined through the paper, and I read it as Bode followed along with his index finger, just like he used to do when learning his favorite Emerson quote.

"May all beings have happiness and the causes of happiness. May all beings be free from suffering and the causes of suffering. May all beings never be parted from freedom's true joy. May all beings dwell in equanimity, free from attachment and aversion."

"Again," he said and rolled onto his side.

By the time I finished reading the poem for the third time, he was asleep with a gentle smile on his face. I kissed his head, and as I flipped off the lamp, I wondered whether the last recitation was for him or me.

seventeen

WE DIDN'T MISS THE sunrise by much. Between the early morning heat and the sunlight illuminating our tent, I had the odd sensation of being roasted like a Thanksgiving turkey. When I opened my eyes, Bode was staring and me and smiling, as if he knew I was about to wake up. "Good morning, Daddy."

"Morning, buddy. How long have you been awake?"

"A little."

"What time is it?" I asked, which was a silly question considering our only clock was on the phone, and it was charging in the truck.

"Time to wake up."

We considered walking to the campground showers but thought better of it. We'd find a hotel somewhere later in the day and figured we could make it until then. We ate a simple breakfast of bagels and bananas before breaking down the tent and cleaning up the site. *Leave No Trace. Leave Only Footprints, Take Only Photographs.* I enjoyed the different mantras employed by campgrounds around the country and thought about them while packing up after each camping trip. My favorite was *Pack it In, Pack it Out*, one I picked up long ago during a trip to Glacier National Park. I would often chant to myself—*pack it in, pack it out, pack it in, pack it out*—after loading up the truck and surveying the campsite one last time, trash bag in hand.

It was still early when we left the campground so I was able to pull the truck close to visitor center without blocking traffic. Bode handed me the phone and with the help of the park's free Wi-Fi, I opened up the map to plan our journey south to Flagstaff. After closing the map, I noticed a new email from Jorge.

> **From:** Jorge Espinoza
> <puntacabras@gmail.com>
> **Date:** August 22, 2023 6:57:12 AM PST
> **To:** Matthew Price
> <matthewprice@me.com>
> **Subject:** Re: Re: Birthday
>
> No, he doesn't share a birthday with Buddha. Don't be ridiculous, Matthew. But he was born the same day the Dalai Lama died. Will you believe me now that there is something special about your boy?

"What's so funny?" Bode asked from his seat in the back.

"Nothing," I said. "Jorge is just being silly."

I pulled out of the lot onto South Entrance Road and then onto East Rim Drive. The sun was still rising in the east, and I lowered the visor and grabbed my sunglasses from the center console. Bode put on his little red sunglasses, too, a pair we'd picked up at The Gap last summer. I asked him if he wanted to move his booster seat behind me to have a better view but he said he was fine.

Though the view was no less spectacular than the day before, I silently berated myself for not appreciating it as much as I had.

We passed signs for Grandview Point and Moran Point but kept driving until we reached Desert View. We parked the truck and walked to the overlook, which instantly restored my appreciation for the natural beauty. The view from the car simply didn't do the Canyon justice and I felt pleased that I was just as awestruck as the day before. I pointed to the Desert View Watchtower and asked Bode if he wanted to climb to the top. He did, so we climbed the eighty-five stairs—he counted—and took in what was arguably the most breathtaking view since our arrival.

Back in the car, I handed the phone to Bode, who plugged it into the charger and the auxiliary jack. I asked him what the DJ had in store for me and he said Amos Lee. "Good choice," I said.

We reached Cameron in about half an hour and turned south. The sun was strong on the left side of my face and arm, and I wondered if it would give me an uneven tan. Bode asked where we were sleeping that night, and I had no answer since I hadn't really planned the journey home. I told him we'd look at the map in Flagstaff and decide over lunch.

We stopped at a Shell station to fill the tank. The reader wasn't reading my card, so I walked inside to pay. I asked the young girl behind the counter if she could recommend somewhere for a quick bite, and she told me about a little pizza joint just up the street. When I returned to the car, Bode had removed the phone from its charger and handed it to me. "You missed a call."

"Did you see who it was?"

"I couldn't read it but I saw 'Price.'"

"Uncle Michael." I tapped on the voicemail and listened to his message. He wanted to know if we were planning on visiting. I texted him: *Just left grand canyon, spotty coverage. Not sure about OH just yet but will call in a day or so.*

I followed the girl's directions up the road and found the pizza place. The parking lot was empty except for an old Toyota pickup with New Jersey plates. I looked at the clock on the dashboard and noticed it was a few minutes before eleven. I half-expected the restaurant to be closed but when I tried the door, it swung open. The man behind the counter sported a humongous belly beneath a white T-shirt that read *How You Doin'?* and one of those white aprons that fit around the waist. He was bald with bushy gray eyebrows and a jolly smile. I immediately thought of the Laughing Buddha, or *Budai* as Jorge called him.

"What can I getcha'?" he shouted.

I ordered three slices and a couple waters.

"I just put in the first pie, so it will be a few minutes. *Dat* okay?" He placed two cups of water on the counter.

I smiled.

"What?" he asked with a grin on his face.

"You called it a pie. Not many people call it that out here, do they?"

"We do where I'm from."

"Jersey," I guessed, recalling the truck's license plate.

"Paramus."

"We're from Connecticut, ourselves."

"Where abouts?"

"I grew up in New York, but this little man was born after his mom and I moved from Manhattan to Westport."

"Westport Pizzeria," he said. "They serve a good slice."

Bode looked up at me and smiled.

"They do. We live two miles away. It's his favorite," I said, nodding toward Bode.

"Next time you're there, tell 'em Tony DiMico sends his regards. They'll know. So . . . what are you boys doing out in these woods?"

"Vacation. On our way back home, actually. We left the Grand Canyon this morning."

"Spending the day in Flag?"

"No, today's a travel day. We were about to look at the map and figure out where we're headed."

"Albuquerque is about five hours. Another hour to Santa Fe."

He removed the pizza from the oven and sliced it into eighths. He slid two slices onto one paper plate, one onto another, and set the two plates on the counter.

"On the house," he said.

I tried to protest, but he waved me away.

Bode and I sat in a booth by the window and studied the map, which confirmed Tony's estimations. I scanned the map for other cities that might have been of interest along our easterly route but only saw Roswell. I calculated the distance to Roswell but eight hours seemed far. I decided to plot out the route from Albuquerque east to see what the following day would have in store for us. It looked like our choice was pretty much limited to Oklahoma City, which would then put us on a path toward St. Louis, Indianapolis, and, as luck would have it, Columbus. I considered calling Uncle Michael and Aunt Mary then, but if it were only a couple hours from the previous night's stopping point we would probably drive right through. I decided to wait to call when I had a better idea of our schedule.

We finished our pizza and tossed the trash in the garbage. Before we left, I pushed a five into the tip jar on the counter and thanked Tony for the pizza.

"Safe journey, boys," he said waving a floured hand.

A few hours east of Flagstaff, I looked to the mirror and saw Bode napping. I smiled at his cramped posture and stretched my own legs and back, briefly taking some weight off my backside. For the first time on the trip, I felt my spirit fade. I found myself thinking of home, our destination, rather than the journey itself. We had been on the road for nearly two weeks and the journey was nearing its end. I resolved to perk up. Carefully, I reached back and unplugged the charger and plugged it in up front before starting the *On the Road* playlist.

"I like this song," Bode said.

I looked to the rearview and smiled. "Me, too," I said and turned it up.

"Hey, Dad." I lowered the volume back down. "Do you think we'll ever see that woman again?"

"Who?"

"The woman from the beach. The one who offered to help us after we almost drowned."

"We didn't almost drown, you monkey."

"You know what I mean."

"What made you think of her?" I asked.

"I don't know. She was very kind. I liked her."

I looked at him in the mirror but remained silent.

And then he said, "She reminded me of Mom."

"She reminded you of Mom? How could—"

"You know what I mean."

"She reminded you of what you think your mom was like?"

He nodded.

"Well, your mom was one of the kindest women I knew, so that makes sense. But there are a lot of women who are kind, buddy. What is it about that woman from the beach?"

Bode shrugged again and all of sudden got shy. "I just liked her, is all. She was pretty, too." He smiled at me in the mirror. "I think you should have talked to her."

"We discussed this," I said, though I wasn't sure if we did.

"Dad—"

"Bode, I'm happy. I really am. Maybe one day I'll meet a woman who I want to spend time with. And if that day ever comes, I'm sure she will be just as kind and pretty as the woman from the beach."

"And Mom?"

"No woman will ever be as kind and pretty as your mom."

Bode smiled, apparently satisfied with my answer or simply wise enough to let the conversation end. After a moment he asked me to turn up the music. We smiled at one another in the mirror as "Drops of Jupiter" began: *Now that she's back in the atmosphere, with drops of Jupiter in her hair; She acts like summer and walks like rain, reminds me that there's a time to change, hey, hey, hey . . .*

eighteen

BY THE TIME WE ROLLED into Albuquerque, it was after seven in the evening, and I was exhausted. I hadn't remembered to pull over and check out hotels, but we were fortunate to have spotted one just off the highway. After showering, Bode and I returned to the lobby and asked the woman at the front desk for a restaurant recommendation. She said that most restaurants in the area were either steakhouses or Mexican.

"*Cheesadillas?*"

When we returned from dinner we changed into our bathing suits and went for a swim. I wasn't feeling up to a cannonball competition, but I was happy to score Bode's jumps from a comfortable position in the jacuzzi with the jets aimed at my lower back.

Bode fell asleep without a story, and I wrote in my journal for a few minutes before my eyes grew heavy. I jotted notes about the canyon and the drive from Flagstaff to Albuquerque, but my thoughts were as empty as the desert. I would never have expected New Mexico to be as arid and bare as Arizona, but it was even more so. There was simply nothing to look at, nothing to make me curious enough to want to Google, nothing to occupy my thoughts. Even Bode had seemed bored and slept for much of the leg. As I slipped in and out of sleep, I despaired at the likelihood of a similar drive in the morning. The sound of another room's door slamming shut roused me sometime after midnight—pen in hand, squiggles on the paper—and I reached to switch off the lamp.

We slept soundly until seven when the clamor and vibrations from a jackhammer reverberated through our room. It must have been coming from outside, I thought, but it was so loud that it sounded like it was coming from the room next door. I peeked through the curtains and sure enough, they were drilling into the ground just outside the next room's window. I wondered if anyone was staying there.

I took a shower and shaved while Bode meditated on the bed. I asked how he could concentrate with all the noise, and he said he wasn't concentrating on anything. I stood there, cleaning my ears with a Q-tip, and wondered how he did it. At the yoga classes I had attended, I found it hard enough to concentrate on my breath when I heard other people breathing next to me. How he could meditate fifteen feet away from a jackhammer was beyond me.

When we hopped in the car after breakfast I plugged in the phone and pushed the charger deep into the cigarette outlet. Apparently it hadn't charged again. I opted for the CD player and selected Sigur Ros' Takk album. Instantly, I conjured the image of the masked gunmen in Baja and felt grateful for our safe passage.

I felt myself longing for Missouri. I had only been to St. Louis a few times—all one-day business trips to visit Anheuser-Busch—so I didn't have any real experience with the city. Earlier, during lunch, I took note of a green patch on the map about an hour southwest of St. Louis. I imagined that it might be a great place to seek out one of those brown and white camping signs alongside the highway, take the next exit and follow signs to an unknown campground. Reward us after three straight travel days.

"Where are we staying tonight?" Bode asked.

"Good question," I said and pulled onto the shoulder to pull up the Marriott website. The phone did not appear to be charging and was down to just 14%. I figured I could buy a new charger but I had about three of them back home. I booked a room at the Renaissance just off the highway in Oklahoma City and turned the phone off to save the battery.

At dinner, I proposed my idea of trying to find a campground the next day. Bode liked it, and we agreed to set out early in the morning so we could be as spontaneous as we'd like in the afternoon.

I ordered the healthiest salad on the menu, complete with fresh spinach, avocado, tomatoes, onions and some kind of crushed nuts. I must not have been drinking enough water because the waiter refilled my glass about six times throughout the meal. Something told me quesadillas would be for dinner the next night, but I took comfort in the fact we'd probably eat like humans again at Michael and Mary's. I made a mental note to call them first thing in the morning.

Later that evening, Bode took gold in our cannonball competition, but I argued it was only because he had practiced in Albuquerque. He told me he would take it easy on me next time and we relaxed in the hot tub until bedtime.

I read him a story called "Goblin Island." It was a short one and the moral was essentially that things don't always work out the way you want them to, but it's best to face adversity and challenges head on rather than run away from them. I was about to ask Bode if he understood the lesson, but it occurred to me that he already demonstrated his understanding—more eloquently, in fact—by quoting Jon Kabat-Zinn days earlier.

I woke early the next morning, feeling refreshed and ready to tackle another seven hours of pavement. Bode was still asleep when I went into the shower but he was dressed and ready to roll when I got out.

We ate breakfast at the hotel, at the same restaurant where we ate dinner. I had no idea what day it was, but it had to be a weekday because businessmen and women surrounded us in the dining room wearing suits of blue, gray and black. Didn't anyone realize how hot it was? I thanked my lucky stars that I was able to wear jeans and a button-down to work most days, and even when we pitched ideas to the stiffest clients they seemed to expect us to be dressed casually. How else could we tap into our creative side? We had them all fooled, but I wasn't going to spill the beans.

While Bode explored the buffet, I picked up the copy of *The New York Times*. The headline on the front page caught my attention: *Tibet's Panchen Lama Emerges After 28-Year Disappearance.* I looked across the dining room toward the flat screen hanging behind the bar. It was quite a ways away, but I was able to make out CNN's logo and a few monks in saffron robes. I glanced at Bode who was scooping fruit into a bowl and then back down at the newspaper.

By the time I finished reading the article, Bode was seated beside me with an empty bowl of yogurt. A few pieces of fruit remained on his plate.

"Are you going to eat, Dad?"

"I am," I said, cutting a wedge from my omelet. "I was just reading this article." I paused a moment to eat a few bites of egg. "Remember we talked about what's going on in China and how the Tibetan monks have been searching for the Dalai Lama's reincarnation?"

"Yeah," he said, dropping a slice of strawberry into his mouth.

"Use your fork, please."

He smiled and lifted his fork.

"Well, the Panchen Lama, the guy who's said to be able to identify the Dalai Lama's incarnation, has just appeared after twenty-eight years."

"Where has he been?"

"He's been missing. Twenty-eight years ago, the Dalai Lama selected a six-year-old boy as the 11th Panchen Lama, Tibet's second highest ranking monk behind the Dalai Lama, himself. A few days later, he was kidnapped and has never been seen since."

"Until now?"

"Until now. Some people think that he's been held captive all these years. Others thought he and his family were killed. The crazy thing is that just a few months after the boy disappeared, China selected a different boy as the Panchen Lama."

"A different one?"

"Yes, this one." I pointed to a picture of Gyaltsen Norbu, who wore frameless glasses and a saffron robe with a floral decoration on the chest.

"Why would they do that?" he asked.

"Control, I guess. Like I said, the Panchen Lama is supposed to help identify the Dalai Lama's incarnation."

"And China wants to find him," Bode said, once again surprising me with his level of understanding.

"Well, that's what I thought, but if the Dalai Lama-appointed Panchen Lama is alive—and free—perhaps not."

Bode chewed a piece of cantaloupe and I watched as his wheels spun. "Is this the one who was kidnapped?" he asked, pointing to a young Gendhun Choekyi Nyima.

"Yes. This is him at six, and this is him now at thirty-four."

"He looks the same," Bode said. "His face didn't really change."

"Well, it's not like he's old," I laughed. "He's my age."

"And he disappeared when he was just six?"

"Mhmm. Maybe China was protecting him after all."

Bode was paying close attention and seemed to be awaiting more of the story. I wasn't sure how much more I had for him.

"Or, perhaps he really was living in hiding," I continued. "Like Chinese authorities have maintained all along."

"Why?"

"I don't know. Maybe to study the sutras? Maybe because his parents didn't want him to be in the spotlight? I have no idea."

Bode finished the last of his fruit. I watched him closely to see if I could read his mind but came up empty. Just before I asked he said, "So, now what?"

"I don't know. The article says he's on his way to New Delhi."

"No, I mean, now what for us? Are we going?"

I smiled and said, "Let me finish my coffee and we'll get out of here."

nineteen

IN MY HASTE TO GET as close to St. Louis as possible, I thought we might have missed our last opportunity to camp before reaching the city. Fortunately, we spotted signs for Meramec State Park about seventy-five miles out, and we followed tree-lined Route 185 to the park's entrance.

It was about four o'clock by the time we checked in and set up camp. I found myself becoming lazier and lazier at each campground, removing fewer necessities like the tent, sleeping bags and pads, and kitchen gear. The trees provided plenty of shade and the picnic table a place to eat, so we left the E Z-Up, tables, and one of the chairs packed away in the truck.

While Bode collected kindling for a fire, I called Michael and Mary to let them know what time we were aiming for the next day. We'd been eight hours from Columbus when we exited the highway, so I figured we had to leave by nine in order to arrive for dinner. Michael was at work when I called, but I spoke to Mary who suggested we take our time. Even so, I didn't want to arrive late and put them out, which reminded me why I'd been reluctant to agree to a visit in the first place.

Bode dropped a pile of twigs and sticks beside the fire ring. He said he'd found a bunch of dry branches and would be right back with another load. I took the time to study the photocopied map of the area that the woman in the park's office handed me when we checked in. As usual, I found myself staring at the map without making any sense of it. Fortunately, the leaflet had trail descriptions with written instructions so all we needed to do was find the trailhead.

Bode returned with another stack of kindling and smiled proudly at the pile.

"Good job, buddy. We'll have a nice fire later."

He removed even more sticks from the pocket of his hoodie and shot me another grin.

"Want to go for a walk?" I asked. "See if we can find any of those caves the woman mentioned?"

We filled our CamelBaks and grabbed our headlamps. I didn't think we'd be out late enough to need the flashlights, but I figured it couldn't hurt, especially if we decided to check out any of the park's caves. Being unfamiliar with the park, I wasn't sure if the trailhead for the River Trail was in walking distance but I was through with driving for the day. Bode was happy to stretch his legs as well, so we took off hoping for the best.

The River Trail was flat and reminiscent of some of our local trails back home in Connecticut. We followed the yellow blazes until we hit the Bluff Trail, which was a bit steeper and brought us atop two rises with fantastic views of the Meramec River. Occasionally, Bode would spot something and ask me what it was. Having only gained an appreciation for nature and the outdoors in my late twenties, I was unfamiliar with the names of most critters. If a bird was blue, it was likely a bluebird or a blue jay. If it was red, perhaps a cardinal. If it scurried on the ground, it was most definitely a chipmunk or squirrel. At the end of the day, if we encountered a bear, would it matter if I knew the difference between *Ursus arctos horriblis* and *Ursus americanus*? I taught Bode what mattered: to run faster than your slowest friend.

Just as I was thinking about bears, on our way back to our campsite we passed a family of four taking a stroll in the campground. The father was carrying the younger of the two children in a carrier on his back and holding his wife's hand. Their son, around six years old, was prancing about dressed in a bear costume. Now, I wasn't usually one to judge the parenting practices others, but a bear costume? *In the woods?* I could only imagine the potential consequences.

Back at camp, Bode and I joked about the costume. He, too, thought it was silly, but for a different reason. While he couldn't fathom anyone shooting a bear, he figured a kid in a bear costume could certainly give others a fright, especially those who are not particularly fond of the great *Ursus americanus.*

Bode asked if Eliza had ever made me wear a bear costume, grizzly or otherwise. He knew his mom loved dressing up—no matter the occasion—and that she had often picked out my costumes to coordinate with her own. As we built a fire, I told Bode more about his mom's proclivity for dressing up and a funny story that ended with a trip to the hospital.

Halloween was the holy grail of holidays for Eliza, and she would invariably host a party each year. Her preparations for the annual shindig would begin weeks in advance. Although she had the preparations down to a science, creating the perfect costume was still a major undertaking, often requiring a combination of online purchases, trips to Michael's, sewing, and most importantly, trial runs.

When we'd first moved to Westport, we only owned one car, and Eliza and I would drive to the train station together each morning, more often than not returning on the same train, too. On the evenings in which one of us needed to work late, the other would come back to the station and wait in the same spot.

One Friday morning in late October, Eliza left a voicemail for her boss, saying she had a ton of work to get done by the end of the day and it would be easier to work from home without the distractions in the office. Of course, she was lying—and her boss undoubtedly knew, considering he and his wife were invited to party each year—but she wasn't completely lying. She did have work to do—on her costume—in preparation for the party the following night.

That evening, I returned home on the 5:48, the train Eliza and I often took together. It had been an awful day at the office, and I'd grabbed a scotch on the platform before hopping on the train. By the time I arrived in Westport, the edge had worn off, and I was feeling good. As I walked toward the parking lot, I spotted two white Land Cruisers across the lot near our designated spot. As I approached, I saw a blonde woman behind the wheel of one, so I instinctively walked to the other, opened the back door, and tossed in my briefcase before climbing into the front.

"Hey baby," I said, leaning over to give Eliza a kiss. "What a day."

"Hold on," she said into her cell phone and turned to me. "Hi handsome, who are you?"

I jumped back so fast that I smacked my head on the top of the passenger side door. The woman burst out laughing, a hand covering her mouth doing little to conceal her amusement.

Unfortunately, her husband was not as quick to understand. After apologizing, I climbed out of the truck and opened the back door to grab my briefcase when a man swung me around by the shoulder and asked what the hell I was doing.

"I got in the wrong car," I said, fearing he was going to take a swing at me.

"*What?*"

"I got in the wrong car," I repeated and motioned toward the other white Land Cruiser. For the first time, I was able to see Eliza's face through the glass. She was laughing hysterically and wearing a blonde wig. When she climbed out of the truck, I saw that she was dressed as Marilyn Monroe in a white, satin halter-top dress and high heels. Laughing with tears running down her cheek—over her fake beauty mark, of course—she explained what had happened. The other woman joined us between the trucks, and we all shared a laugh, despite the blood gushing from my scalp. Eliza, of course, invited the couple to our party before taking me to the emergency room for eight stitches.

It wasn't until Bode had stopped laughing that I became aware of music coming from an adjacent campsite. A group of college kids were blasting music from their car while they set up camp. I cringed at the thought of hearing music all night but was quick to remember that it wasn't so long since my friends and I probably drove other people crazy with similar behavior.

Over dinner—hopefully the last quesadilla that I will ever eat—I asked Bode what he wanted to be for Halloween. He said he wasn't sure but was pretty adamant about not wanting another full-body costume from Old Navy.

"You didn't like the chicken costume?" I asked.

"I don't really remember that one."

"I have pictures," I said with a smile.

Bode gave me the evil eye.

"How about the cow?"

"You're funny, Dad."

"The udders were funny," I said and tickled his belly. "I guess you can always be a bear. Should we ask that boy where he got his suit?"

"Funny, Dad."

After dinner, we tossed the remaining wood into the fire. Bode lay on me, as I stretched out and rested my heels on the fire ring. We sat quietly, staring at the rippling flames and listening to the snaps, crackles, and pops of our final campfire. Later in the tent, Bode practiced reading Jorge's poem while I attempted to write in my journal. I must have nodded off quickly because when I woke after midnight—the overhead light bronzing with dying batteries—I had only written two sentences.

We woke early and decided to hit the road before breakfast to avoid rush hour traffic. I wasn't certain St. Louis actually had rush hour traffic, but as a New Yorker it was something I considered almost subconsciously, like gas in the tank. It was just after eight when we passed through the city, and I asked Bode if he wanted to stop for breakfast. He said the granola bar he ate earlier was enough, and he'd be fine until lunch. All morning I tried to recall the name of a restaurant in Indianapolis I'd lunched at years before while on a business trip. I remembered the address though—888 Massachusetts Avenue—and after programming the GPS, I was pleased to find R Bistro still open for business when we arrived just after noon. We joked about how there was no quesadilla on the menu and how difficult that made it to choose from the wide selection of entrees.

Back in the car after lunch, I called Michael and Mary and left a message on their home voicemail with an ETA of four o'clock. When I hung up, Bode was turned around and reaching into the back of the truck. I asked him what he was looking for and he said his hoodie with the *vajra*. As he fumbled around in the back, I checked out CNN on the phone to see what was going on in the world: a 6.4 magnitude earthquake had struck New Zealand; Christian and Emily were spotted together in Lake Como (weren't they just in L.A.?); the Yankees were surprisingly just two back of the wildcard; the Panchen Lama and his entourage were seen at the Delta Terminal at New Delhi's airport.

"Found it," Bode said and climbed back into his booster seat.

I put the phone on standby and plugged it into the charger. It had been plugged in all morning, but the battery was at a paltry 8%. I pressed firmly on the adapter, but the phone refused to recognize the charger. It was toast, I figured, but we'd be home in a day. I could manage without a phone for twenty-four hours, couldn't I? As I fired up the engine, I wondered how long it had been since I pulled off such a feat.

After merging onto I-70, I spotted Bode meditating in the rearview. He looked so peaceful as his body bounced along with the rhythm of the truck. I took the time to reflect on our trip and felt supremely grateful for having had nearly three weeks alone with my little man. I felt a little guilty, however, for allowing my thoughts to wander those last few days. Thoughts of home—my bed, my new job, Bode starting first grade, when the lawn was last watered, cooking a proper meal for Bode and Naja—so many trivial thoughts, I lamented. There was so much to appreciate those last few days, yet I found myself longing for the tedious future.

I felt like talking, so once Bode finished meditating I explained how the U.S. highways were numbered. I told him how east-west highways were even-numbered while north-south ones were odd-numbered. He didn't seem completely uninterested so I went on to explain how the numbers started low in the south and west and went up as you traveled north and east. I told him that I used to think that one of every five miles of U.S. highway was straight—so an airplane could land in an emergency—but that turned out to be urban legend. He said he thought it made sense, though, and I couldn't disagree.

We arrived in Columbus at about half past three and followed the GPS directions to Michael and Mary's house in New Albany. It was an affluent town, and the directions from the navigation system were consistent with street signs pointing us to the New Albany Country Club.

No cars were parked on the street, so I turned into Michael and Mary's driveway and pulled behind a navy BMW SUV. A white BMW sedan was parked in a garage that remained open. Bode and I climbed out of the truck and, as I grabbed our duffle from the back, I looked at the house next door and then across the street. Each was a mini mansion—brick Georgian estates with sash windows and white columns surrounding the entryway—and unique only in their shape and color of the shudders.

I banged on the brass knocker that looked too small to make much noise but within seconds Aunt Mary opened the door.

"Hey guys, welcome!" she said and gave me a hug. "It's so nice to see you. Come in, come in."

Bode asked to use the restroom and Mary showed him to the half bath just inside the front door. She told me that Michael had just come home—he left work early—but was upstairs in the shower and would be right down. As she spoke, I couldn't help notice the size of her diamond earrings. She looked much younger than the fifty-five-year-old woman I'd expected to see. Everything was tight and lifted and made me think that perhaps money *can* buy happiness. If not happiness, certainly fake breasts and Botox.

Bode came out of the bathroom looking relieved.

"Let me take a look at you. You look so much older than the pictures I've seen," Mary said, and I wondered which pictures she had seen. Bode and I followed her to the kitchen where she was in the middle of preparing a salad. Apparently Michael had suggested we go out, but she figured we could use a home-cooked meal and baked spinach lasagna for us instead.

"How are the kids?" I asked, finally getting a word in.

"They're wonderful, thank you. Shannon is living in Portland and working for Nike as a graphic designer, and you just missed Mark. He left Wednesday to head back to Boulder."

"What day is it?" I asked.

Mary smiled and said it was Friday, before offering us a drink.

Bode asked for a pineapple juice and, to my astonishment, Mary had a half-gallon tin in the cupboard. I gave Bode's head a rub and he looked up at me smiling. I gratefully accepted a glass of wine from a bottle Mary had opened moments before we arrived. Bode and I sat on bar stools at the granite island while Mary tended to the salad. She noticed Bode staring as she chopped a cucumber, so she put a handful on a side dish and slid it in front of him. He happily began picking as Mary chopped more veggies, occasionally placing extras on the dish.

"My kids still don't eat their vegetables," she laughed.

"This one can't get enough," I said and stood to greet Michael, who entered wearing jeans and a crisp button-down shirt.

"There he is! How are you, Matthew?" his voice echoed through the room.

"I'm fine, thank you. It's good to see you." I gave him a hug. "This is Bode. Bode, come say hi to Uncle Michael."

"Hi, Uncle Michael."

"Hi, handsome. It's nice to finally meet you. Have you enjoyed your trip with your dad so far?"

Bode grew a bit bashful, perhaps a consequence of Uncle

Michael's booming voice, but nodded. Uncle Michael asked if everyone was hungry. I didn't think Bode would be too hungry just yet—we had eaten only a few hours ago—but I said we were and that the lasagna smelled delicious.

We followed him into the living room and took a seat on the couch. Bode placed his glass on a coaster on the coffee table and climbed onto my lap.

"Your dad tells me you're about to start first grade. Are you excited?"

Bode nodded.

"Are you being shy, mister? Uncle Michael is talking to you."

Bode smiled. "I'm going to miss my kindergarten teacher."

"I can imagine. But I'm sure your first grade teacher is going to be great. I still remember mine," Michael said.

"Me, too," I added.

"Mine wore purple slippers," Mary said, entering the living room with a serving plate of cheese and crackers in one hand and her wine in the other.

Bode smiled and we all laughed.

"I'm serious," Mary said. "After lunch and before rest hour, we helped her out of her shoes and into her purple slippers. We would argue over who got to help her each day."

Bode asked, "Did you have to take a nap?"

"I don't remember," Mary said, "but we had quiet time."

"I'm sure they'll let you meditate," I said. "You won't have to nap if you don't want to."

"Meditate? You meditate?" Michael bellowed.

Bode nodded.

"That's excellent," Mary said. "I think all kids should."

"He's been practicing yoga, too," I said, and Bode turned his face into my chest. "Naja, our au pair, has been practicing with him. He's gotten really good." I gave his shoulder a little squeeze. "Naja wants to take you to classes with her. What do you think?"

Bode shrugged and then rubbed his eyes.

"Are you tired, sweetheart?" Mary asked.

Bode shrugged again.

"He's just being shy. Hey, Michael, didn't you used to play chess?"

"Sure. I played all through high school and into college. I taught the kids to play, too. Mark was in the chess club in high school. He can take me about half the time these days."

"How old was he when you taught him?" I asked. "Bode started playing last year."

"He must of have been around Bode's age," Mary answered. "You'd already taught Shannon to play, right?"

"They must have both been around four or five," Michael decided. "Would you like to play after dinner?"

Bode nodded enthusiastically.

"He's been dying to play. We have it on the phone but it's too hard to concentrate with the small screen. We haven't played since the night before we left home."

"We'll play after dinner. How does that sound?" Michael said.

"Okay."

I rubbed Bode's head and excused myself for a minute. When I returned to the living room, Bode was kneeling beside the coffee table and helping himself to some cheese and crackers. Mary looked at me and mouthed, *he's adorable,* and I said that he looked just like his mom.

Bode devoured Mary's spinach lasagna. After she'd served him a huge portion, he helped himself to a second nearly as large as the first. Michael and Mary were gracious hosts; they were quick to fill our glasses and were eager to learn all about Bode and what our lives were like in Connecticut. I told them all about our adventures together and updated them on my new job. Michael admitted that they never paid much attention to marketing at his software company, but he suggested I call his vice president after I settled into my new role to see if they could throw some business our way. Michael's small company, as he modestly referred to it, pulled in about $20 million a year. Not bad for a twelve-person company.

After we cleared the table, Michael went to find the chess set. From the kitchen, Mary offered to brew some coffee but Michael and I opted to stick with wine. Mary brought out some milk for Bode and placed a plate of bakery cookies in the middle of the table, but slid them a hair toward Bode.

Bode choose to be black as usual. I acted as a consultant for him as he took on Uncle Michael. Mary sat beside her husband but smiled at Bode the entire time. Bode was clearly concentrating heavily on the match and absently eating one cookie after another. Watching the two of them play must have brought back fond memories for Mary, who seemed content to watch game after game. In all, they played three games, none of which Bode won, but he went down swinging in each.

"Remember, you want to control the center of the board. That's the key."

Bode looked at me and smiled. It's the advice I had been giving him for months.

"Got it?"

He nodded.

"Okay, well I hope to play again before too long. Mary and I will be in New York this fall. Maybe we can see you then and have a rematch."

"Okay," he said over a yawn.

I asked Bode to get ready for bed, and while he was gone, Michael and Mary complimented me on how wonderful he was and what I great job I was doing. I allowed Michael to fill my glass one last time.

Bode went to sleep in Mark's room without a story, and I rejoined Michael and Mary. I can't say it was a surprise when the topic of conversation turned to my personal life. I explained that there were no girlfriends, that I had my hands full with work and Bode. Michael shushed me with a dismissive wave and a "Hogwash." After letting him go on for few minutes, I intimated that I just wasn't ready to move on.

Mary gave a compassionate smile and pinched Michael on the arm while whispering, "That's enough."

Before saying good night, I thanked them for a wonderful evening. Outside the guest room, I reminded them that Bode and I were planning on making it home the next day—eleven hours—so we would be leaving pretty early. Mary asked what pretty early was and I said, "Sevenish."

"We'll be up," Michael said with the first trace of alcohol showing in his speech.

"We haven't slept past six in twenty years," Mary added. "We'll wake you. Unless you wake up from Michael at his computer first."

Michael patted Mary on her backside and started down the hall toward the master bedroom. "Good night, my nephew," he called with a wave over his shoulder.

"No more wine for him," Mary said and hugged me good night.

As I undressed in the guest room, I thought to charge the phone, but the wall charger was in the truck. Before placing the phone on the nightstand, I noticed a new voicemail from a 203 number. Curious, I clicked on the message as I sat on the bed.

"Hi there," said a soft-spoken voice. "You probably don't remember me, but we met briefly at the beach a few weeks ago. Your adorable son accidentally left his lunch bag behind, and it had your number on it. I wanted to call earlier, but I had to travel unexpectedly and just returned home. Your son is probably starting school next week, so if you'd like it back, give me a—"

The battery died.

I sat for a moment with the dead phone in my hands. For the first time in years, I felt what were probably butterflies in my stomach. I also realized that I hadn't taken a breath since the message began. I placed the phone on the nightstand and crawled under the covers.

"*Accidentally*," I said to myself, as I switched off the lamp. "That little shit."

twenty

TRUE TO MARY'S WORD, she and Michael had been awake at the crack of dawn. The smell of freshly brewed coffee seeped its way into the guest room along with the sound of Michael's fingers banging away on his keyboard. Not even 6:30 on a Saturday, and he was at it.

I took a quick shower before waking Bode and had him take one as well. Michael was laughing at something on his monitor when I walked by and said good morning. I sauntered into the kitchen and took a seat at the island where Mary poured me a cup of coffee. I sat quietly for a moment, staring as the cream swirled into the coffee. I became acutely aware of all the sounds in the house: Bode's shower, NPR on the radio, Michael's printer and the sound of his chair rolling across hardwood floor, the post-brewing drips of the coffee machine, Mary's slippers.

"I think I'm a little hung over."

Mary placed a hand on my shoulder. "Advil?"

"That'd be great," I said, massaging my temples with my fingers.

Michael walked into the kitchen, already showered and dressed like he was ready to hit the links. He set a piece of paper beside my coffee.

"I'm not a fan of chain emails," he said, "but it's the only way I know that my Aunt Barbara is alive. She forwards every email she gets, and I don't have the heart to ask her to remove me from her distribution list."

"Be nice," Mary said as she filled his mug and handed me a bottle of Advil.

The subject of the email read, "The Arrogance of Authority." I swallowed two pills and read the email:

> *A DEA officer stopped at a ranch in Texas and met with the old rancher.*
>
> *"I need to inspect your ranch for illegally-grown drugs," said the officer.*
>
> *The rancher replied, "Okay, but whatever you do, don't go in that field over there."*
>
> *The DEA officer shouted, "Sir, I have the authority of the Federal Government." He reached into his pocket, pulled out his badge, and shoved it in the old rancher's face. "See this badge? This badge means I am allowed to go wherever I want, whenever I want. No questions asked or answers given. Have I made myself clear?"*
>
> *The rancher nodded politely, apologized and went about his chores.*
>
> *A short time later, the old rancher heard loud screams. He looked up to see the DEA officer running for his life, chased by a 2,000-pound Santa Gertrudis bull. With every step the bull was gaining*

> *ground on the terrified officer and it seemed likely that he'd be gored before reaching the safety of the wood fence.*
>
> *The rancher threw down his tools, ran toward the fence, and yelled at the top of his lungs: "Your badge! Show him your badge!"*

Fortunately, only a little coffee came out my nose when I burst out laughing, which made Michael spit up coffee in his own mug.

"Gentlemen!" Mary cried as she tore off a paper towel off from the spool beside the sink.

Bode walked in dressed in bright orange cargo shorts, a white polo T-shirt and green Crocs.

"Don't you look handsome," Mary said.

"Hi."

"What do you say?" I asked.

"Thank you," Bode said. And then, "Good morning," unsure which response I was expecting.

"Would you like some breakfast?" Mary asked.

"Yes, please," he said.

"What good manners," she said and Bode flashed me a smile. "I can make eggs if you'd like. There's also some fruit and yogurt on the table. I have cereal, too."

"Fruit and yogurt, please."

We migrated to the dining room. The table was already set for four with orange juice in each glass and a newspaper folded beside Michael's plate. I marveled at Mary's attention to detail: the towels that had been laid out on the beds; a brand new bar of soap atop each pile; a bottle of water on our nightstands; breakfast; the newspaper. Michael was a lucky man, it seemed, though he was no slouch himself. I wondered if it was all show. I'd grown fond of them during our short visit and certainly hoped they were as happy as they seemed.

As Michael unfolded the newspaper, I caught a glimpse of the front page. Several monks—possibly even the Panchen Lamas we read about yesterday—were photographed in the Arrivals hallway of some airport. One of them was holding a bottle of Poland Spring, which for some reason I found amusing.

"Honey, not while we have company," Mary said.

Michael smiled apologetically, folded the paper, and set it down.

I didn't want to eat and run, but we had a long drive ahead of us. Michael and Mary didn't pressure us to stay, for which I was grateful. It turned out that Michael had an early tee time and Mary was heading to an eight o'clock *vinyasa* class. As we finished up, Mary filled a to-go cup of coffee for me and handed Bode a small lululemon athletica bag filled with bottled water and snacks. We thanked them for their hospitality, said our goodbyes, and hit the road just after seven. As we were pulling out of the driveway, Bode spotted Mary running out of the house.

"You forgot this!" she said, holding out my phone.

"Thank you," I said, taking the dead phone and tossing it into an empty cup holder.

Bode slept for much of the morning leg but woke as I pulled off the highway for gas.

"Are we almost home?" he asked after I climbed back into the truck and pulled onto the highway.

"Not quite," I said. "You weren't sleeping that long."

"Why does it say 'New York City' then?"

Pleased with his reading skills, I told him that we were getting onto I-80, which would take us through Pennsylvania, New Jersey, and New York before arriving in Connecticut.

"Not Pennsylvania again."

I looked to the rearview and smiled, recalling how driving through Pennsylvania had seemed to take forever when we first set out on our trip. About twenty minutes later I pointed out the big blue sign on the side of the highway.

"Pennsylvania welcomes you, buddy."

He scrunched his nose at me in the mirror. "How many states today?"

I counted in my head. "Five."

"Is that our most?"

"I think we did seven our first day, didn't we?"

"Connecticut, New York, Pennsylvania—"

"Don't forget New Jersey."

"Then what?"

"After Pennsylvania? Maryland, West Virginia, and Virginia, right?"

He nodded and then frowned as he thought of something.

"What?"

"It rained so much then."

"It certainly did."

Pennsylvania did seem like the longest part of the drive. Interstate 80 went on forever, and though there were signs to Pittsburgh and eventually Harrisburg and Allentown, driving 300 miles without passing a single recognizable city was mind numbing. According to the GPS, we had exactly 200 miles to go when we exited the highway for lunch in Bloomsburg, PA. My hangover was gone, but so was my coffee, and after seven hours behind the wheel I was in desperate need of more.

We grabbed a quick bite and filled the tank one final time. As we approached New Jersey, I began to feel anxiety for the first time in weeks. Was there traffic ahead? What day, exactly, was Barcott expecting me in the office? Did I owe him a call? Would I be able to hold it together when I put Bode on the bus for the first time? Which bills were not on auto-pay? Had I paid Naja recently?

I considered calling Naja to let her know we were just over an hour from home but remembered the phone was dead. Bode asked me to turn on the radio and for the first time in more than two weeks, the presets tuned into static-free stations. I scrolled through a few that were playing commercials until I found one with music.

We're all walking on quicksand.
When we're busy makin' our plans, God laughs.

Isn't that the truth, I thought. It made me think of Eliza and the life we had planned for ourselves. I thought about her decision to move forward with the pregnancy and postpone her treatment six months. *It's not too late,* the doctors had protested. *You can always have another child.* Eliza wouldn't hear it. She was going to have her child—*this child*—even if it killed her. I looked at Bode in the mirror and smiled. He caught my gaze and gave me a knowing smile in return.

We're all walking on quicksand.
When we're busy makin' our plans, God laughs.

I thought about my parents and how God, Fate, the Universe got it all wrong. How it was supposed to have been the teenager driving home from his SAT prep course to run the red light and smash into the doctor and his wife, not the other way around. How my father should never have been driving the night in which he was being honored and how they should have just arranged for a car. I opened the windows and turned the radio up. We were about to go over the Tappan Zee Bridge, and I shared the only fact I knew about Nyack.

"Hey, you know that painting your mom bought me?"

"The one of the diner?"

"The artist was born in this town," I said, nodding to the left.

"How do you know?"

"I love that painting. It's one of my favorites."

"Because Mom bought it for you?"

"Yeah, but there's more to the story. After your mom and I moved to Westport, we took a memoir writing class together at Staples High School."

"What's a memoir?"

"A memoir is a story about a certain time or event in your life," I said, moving into the left lane and speeding up. We were less than an hour from home and I was getting excited.

"Like your journal?"

"Exactly. I didn't want to go, but your mom insisted. It was either that or a cooking class."

"You like to cook."

"Yes, well, now I do. I've had to learn, but your mom was a much better cook than me back then. I *really* didn't want to cook so we agreed on the memoir writing class. Anyway, one of the exercises the instructor had us do was write a description of one of several paintings."

"You chose the one in the guest room?"

"It's called *Nighthawks*, by an artist named Edward Hopper. He's from Nyack, the town we just passed."

"What'd you write?"

"I described it as an all-night diner in the 1940s or so and that the people looked very disconnected. I made up a story about why the man was alone and how the couple was at a crossroads in their relationship. I said something about the lighting and how it spilled onto the street, and that actually turned out to be one of the important attributes of painting. Your mom joked that I should have been an art history major. It became a running joke each time we saw a painting in a museum or someone's home. She would ask me to describe it because I, apparently, *understood* art. I'm really bad at it, actually, but that night in our class, I was put on the spot and got lucky."

"I like that painting, too," Bode said.

"You do?"

He nodded.

"Why do you like it?" I asked.

"Because Mom bought it for you," he smiled. "The painting, itself, seems a little . . ."

"Dark?"

"Yeah."

"It is, that's kind of the point of it, though. I like it mostly because it reminds me of taking that class with your mom."

It was almost six in the evening on Saturday and traffic was getting heavy on the other side of I-287 heading into the city. When we took the curve to the left onto I-95, it felt like we were on the homestretch, with just over twenty miles to go. Oncoming traffic was bumper-to-bumper, and I hoped that once we hit Exit 3, the first exit in Connecticut, we, too, wouldn't hit traffic as we so often did. The sun was starting its descent behind us and it was getting difficult to see Bode with the sunlight sneaking in the back window above the packed-down camping gear.

The heat and high humidity of the late August day seemed

like it had gotten worse once we entered Connecticut, and I wondered why we chose to live in the Northeast. The winters were dreadfully cold, summers oppressively hot and humid. Why did we do it to ourselves? When the time came, I mused, perhaps Bode would choose USC and I would follow him out west.

It was a long day, and we were sweaty as it was, so I left the windows and sunroof open, which provided something of a breeze when traffic moved. It slowed at Exit 3 in Greenwich but kept pace, slowed in Stamford, picked up in Darien, slowed again in Norwalk, and then finally opened up after Exit 15, allowing me to open up the engine for the final two miles to our exit.

After exiting the highway, I looked at Bode in the rearview as I came to a stop at the red light at Park and Riverside, adjacent the I-95 overpass. I asked how he felt.

"Okay."

"Are you glad to be home?"

"I guess."

"Did you have fun?" I asked.

"Yes."

The light turned green, and I made the left onto Riverside, then a right onto Bridge Street. We passed a few restaurants, which reminded me that we'd probably want to eat something when we got home. I hadn't expected Naja to do a food shopping and figured there wasn't much in the refrigerator.

"Hey, Dad?"

"Yeah, buddy," I said as I pulled up to the stoplight facing Compo Road South.

"Thank you."

"For what?"

"For everything. For taking me on vacation. I had *a lot* of fun."

I reached behind and gave his knee a squeeze. "You're welcome," I said. "Thank you for being such a great co-pilot. I had lots of fun, too." The light turned green and I turned left on Compo Road South. "Are you hungry?" I asked as we stopped at another light at the Post Road.

Bode nodded.

"What are you in the mood for? There's probably not much in the house."

"I don't know. Maybe Chinese?"

"That sounds good. Maybe we'll order from The Little Kitchen," I said, gesturing toward shopping center across the street. In the rearview, I spotted Bode rubbing his temple with his fingers. "What's wrong?"

"This is the light."

"What light?"

"Whaddayacallit?"

"The intersection?" I asked.

"Yeah."

"The one where you feel the energy?"

He nodded.

"Can you feel it now?"

Another nod.

"Hmm. Well, the light will change in just a second," I said.

"A hundred seconds."

"What?"

"It will change in a hundred more seconds. It's a hundred-eighty seconds on Saturdays."

"Are you serious?"

He nodded and then gave me a little smile. I could tell he was keeping count in his head.

"What are you at now?"

"A hundred-fifty but you made me lose count."

Another thirty seconds passed, and the light finally turned green. I looked at him in the mirror and asked, "What's it on weekdays?"

"Two hundred-forty."

We crossed the Post Road and passed Winslow Park on our left. Out of habit, we both gazed over the three-foot stone wall into the park to see if we could spot any dogs walking the loop. I spotted a golden and saw that Bode had as well.

"Hey, Dad, can I see the phone?"

"We're almost home, buddy. Plus, it's dead. The charger's broken." And then I realized something. I unplugged the adapter from the cigarette charger and handed it to Bode. "Try plugging it in back there."

Bode took the phone and charger and plugged it in.

Immediately, the phone chimed indicating that the charger was working.

"The screen turned on," he said.

"I guess the charger is fine after all. It's probably just a blown fuse."

"A what?"

"I'm just talking to myself. Why don't you power it on?" A minute later, we were at the blinking red light at Cross Highway, the street that borders our development. We were three-quarters of a mile from home. I turned right and the phone sounded three different types of chimes indicating voicemail, email, and text messages.

"Sounds like church bells," I said.

"I think you have some missed calls or something."

Bode held up the phone for me to see, but I didn't want to turn back while driving. As we approached Hockanum Road, however, there was a hold up, and we came to a standstill a few car-lengths away from our turn. There was a police officer directing traffic into and out of our usually quiet development.

I took the phone from Bode and looked at all the indicators: twenty-eight missed calls, twenty-three voicemails, fourteen text messages, eight emails. *What the hell is going on?* Did our house burn down? The phone was only off for one day. The two cars ahead of us continued straight after a quick word with the officer standing in the middle of the intersection. When we reached him, I asked what was happening.

"Please continue straight on Cross Highway," he answered without even looking at me. It seemed as if he had been asked what's going on one too many times.

"We live here," I said. "We're just getting back from vacation, and I'd like to get home."

He looked at me and said, "Mr. Price?"

"Yes, why?"

"Go on then," the officer said and stepped aside while mumbling something into his radio.

I tossed the phone onto the passenger seat and turned slowly onto Hockanum Road, a very narrow side street. When two cars approach from opposite directions—which almost never happens—both need to slow down and hug the side of the road to pass safely.

I turned into the left side of the street because the right was lined with cars, as if someone was having a backyard bash and guests parked anywhere they could. I drove the hundred yards to the T at the beginning of our street and wondered what was going on and how the officer had known my name. I seriously hoped the house hadn't burn down. If it had, people wouldn't come by to watch, would they?

I veered right on Gault Park Drive. If I had turned left, I would have remained on Hockanum, but it would have turned into Gault Park Drive after just a few houses, since Hockanum Road and Gault Park Drive form a three-quarter mile loop. I idled along, my foot covering the brake. There were people everywhere. Front lawns extended to the street—we had no sidewalks in our development—so everyone was either walking in the street or across peoples' lawns. There were fourteen houses situated around the loop with approximately fourteen more on the opposite side of the street. By the look of it, the entire neighborhood was outside. There must have been more than a hundred people, most walking in the same direction as us.

And then we passed the media vans. One after another—ABC 7, CBS 2, NBC 4, FOX 5, FOX CT, PIX 11, Channel 12—parked along the side with satellite dishes extended high into the trees. I bent forward over the steering wheel to see how high they reached. I turned back to Bode who was staring out the window with his mouth wide open. In my side mirrors I saw neighbors jogging to keep up with us.

The road curved left, and our house came into view. There were two police cars, one on each side of the street, forcing me even slower. Another police car was in our driveway, parked behind a black Cadillac Escalade. I didn't see the Honda I had purchased for Naja, so she was either not home or had parked in the garage.

An officer at the foot of the driveway approached my door. "Mr. Price?"

I nodded.

He stepped aside to allow me to pull in.

In my side mirror I saw him bring his radio to his mouth. I pulled into the driveway and parked beside the Escalade. I was utterly confused. Bode saw them first.

"What the—" he said from the back.

"I have no idea."

I put the truck in park and sat motionless for what could have been a minute or an eternity. I didn't even realize that Bode had gotten out of the truck until he knocked on my window. I opened the door, climbed out, and took hold of his extended hand, as we started up the path toward the house.

Five monks dressed in saffron and gold robes were waiting for us on the porch. The two standing next to the front door wore a combination of maroon and gold cloths, wrapped immaculately around their bodies and covering much of their arms. Both men appeared to be about my age, and the shorter of the two wore frameless glasses and had a floral pattern on the right side of his robe. The taller monk wore a similar robe, but did not have a floral pattern embroidered on the chest. I recognized these two young men immediately as the Panchen Lamas, who were together for perhaps the first time.

Two other monks were leaning against the white columns on the porch and another was seated on the second step. These three wore similar maroon-colored robes, with less yellow exposed, but also flawlessly wrapped. The monk who was sitting on the step appeared to have forty years on all the others.

Bode and I walked halfway up the path and stopped, which somehow felt natural. It was perhaps similar, I thought, to how Anne felt when giving Eliza to me on our wedding day. The five men stepped off the porch and stood facing us. There had to be more than a hundred neighbors, television reporters, police officers, babies, and dogs standing not forty feet behind me but I couldn't hear the slightest sound above the pounding of adrenaline between my ears.

Bode let go of my hand and walked toward the monks, stopping a few feet before the eldest. The old monk—whom I later learned was the 14th Shamarpa, Mipham Chokyi Lodro, the second highest teacher in the Karma Kagyu sect of Tibetan Buddhism behind only the Karmapa—regarded Bode for a moment. Bode's gaze fell to the ground before the monk's feet. The old man, who appeared to be missing his central incisors, smiled a toothless, beneficent smile and turned to the two monks immediately behind him before also nodding toward the ground. These two monks, I later learned, were both enthroned as the 17th Karmapa in yet another controversy, and were certainly standing together for the first time. They stepped forward, placed their palms together, and bowed to Bode and then to me. For the first time, I noticed Naja standing between the family room curtains, crying and laughing into her hands.

The two Karmapas stepped aside, and then two Panchen Lamas stepped forward. With gentle smiles on their faces, they pressed their palms together and bowed to Bode and then to me.

"*Namaste*," Gendhun Choekyi Nyima said. "The light within me honors the light within you."

"*Namaste*," Gyaltsen Norbu repeated.

And then, slowly and deliberately, Bode pressed his own palms together and bowed to the lamas. With his head down and eyes closed, he said, "*Namaste*." Slowly, he stood upright and opened his eyes and smiled. "How did you find me?"

afterword

From: puntacabras@gmail.com
Date: August 23, 2023 1:10:05 AM PST
To: ohhdl@dalailama.com
Subject: IMPORTANT

To Whom It May Concern:

I understand that before his death, the 14th Dalai Lama made a variety of assertions about the likelihood of his incarnation being found outside of the Himalayan region. As such, there is a young boy in America of whom you should be aware.

He lives in the town of Westport, Connecticut and is currently traveling home after a visit to me in Baja California, Mexico. I have become fascinated with this boy after his father, a close friend of mine, introduced me during their recent visit. Since their departure, I have done a great deal of research and have found extraordinary parallels between this young boy, the Supreme Buddha, Siddhartha Gautama, and the late Dalai Lama, Tenzin Gyatso.

Below is an account of what I have learned thus far:

The boy, five years old, was born on December 23, 2017, the same day as His Holiness Tenzin Gyatso's death.

His name, Hubert "Bode" Price, has special meaning. His given name, Hubert, comes from the German elements *hugu*, meaning *heart, mind, spirit*, and *berht*, meaning *bright, famous*. His middle, and preferred moniker, Bode, is derived from the Old English *bodian* or *boda* meaning *messenger*. Bode, which is pronounced *boh-dee*, is also a homonym of the Sanskrit word *bodhi* which, as you know, translates as *enlightenment* or, more literally, *awakening*. His parents were unaware of the meaning of these names when they named their son.

Bode Price was born outside, beneath a tree, in similar circumstances as the Supreme Buddha, Siddhartha Gautama.

Bode's mother died just days after his birth, also like Siddhartha Gautama's mother.

Without encouragement from his father, Bode meditates daily and enjoys practicing yoga. And without any known training, the boy performs Reiki healing/energy work on a variety of animals.

Bode's disposition is one of calm,
peacefulness and compassion unlike
anything I have ever seen in a child.

I urge you to investigate this matter further
and meet Bode Price without delay. Bode
and his father, Matthew Price, reside on
Gault Park Drive, Westport, CT, USA.

Namaste,

Jorge Espinoza
Punta Cabras
Baja, California
Mexico

CPSIA information can be obtained at www.ICGtesting.com
Printed in the USA
BVOW05s1448290515

402346BV00001B/1/P

9 780692 358375